A
DOUBLE
WRONG

A
DOUBLE
WRONG

*A Story About the Dangers of Political Correctness
and Limiting Free Speech*

Leith Harte

ISBN: 978-1-9162199-0-8

DEDICATION

This book was written with inspiration and ideas from my wife, my children, my friends, my teachers, and all people brave enough to speak out in the face of hostility across the world and through the ages.

The people, places, and events in this story are fictional. Some historical events are quoted to provide context for the story. Facts and timescales have been altered for narrative effect. All inaccuracies are my responsibility.

"To suppress free speech is a double wrong. It violates the rights of the hearer as well as those of the speaker."
Frederick Douglass, 1880

CONTENTS

CHAPTER 1

ORDINATION

To Be Sold. A cargo of three hundred prime young negroes.
   —*South Carolina General Gazette,* 1769

No Irish. No Blacks. No Dogs.
   —Sign posted in window of bed and breakfast accommodation, England, 1960

A term of imprisonment of not less than two years.
   —The sentence for gross indecency, which was interpreted by British courts as applying to male homosexual acts. British criminal law, 1885. Repealed in 1967

Here is a decent, ordinary fellow Englishman, who in broad day light in my own town says to me, his member of Parliament, that the country will not be worth living in for his children. I simply do not have the right to shrug my shoulders and think about something else. What he is saying, thousands and hundreds of thousands are saying and thinking— not throughout Great Britain, perhaps, but in the areas that are already undergoing the total transformation to which there is no parallel in a thousand years of English history. We must be mad, literally mad, as a nation to be permitting the annual inflow of some fifty thousand dependents, who are for the most part the material of the future growth of the immigrant-descended population. It is like watching a nation busily engaged in heaping up its own funeral pyre.

   —Enoch Powell, British member of Parliament, in a 1968 speech

Our tale begins in Selchester, a small cathedral city in southeast England, in the second half of the twentieth century.

The beautiful white Norman cathedral in Selchester was built at great expense in 1075 by conquering Norman warlords led by William of Normandy. With white stone shipped from Normandy by sea, it still stands as a monument to ancient and traditional Christian values. The green squares of Selchester College of Theology have existed for a mere two hundred years by comparison. Nevertheless, the current students of Selchester College might sense a real presence of antiquity during their three years of theology training.

The chapel bells at Selchester College of Theology peeled in joyous celebration on a beautiful June day. Over one hundred new Anglican priests were being ordained in Selchester Cathedral and released on an unsuspecting public. How great were God and his wonderful works to have provided such a group of enthusiastic new recruits!

The ordinands (i.e., newly qualified priests) were all dressed in their official vestments for their ordination. These were the formal uniforms that they were to wear when discharging their sacred duties. These included their cassock (black ankle-length coat), stole (coloured scarf), alb (white coat), and white clerical collar. They looked quite a picture.

Father Joseph Sage was one of the older ordinands on this bright and sunny summer day in Selchester. Father Sage mixed with his fellow ordinands, their friends, and their families.

The diocese of Selchester in England has existed for almost a thousand years. A diocese, which is sometimes called a bishopric, is a district under the care of a bishop. The original diocese was founded in the seventh century at Sealsey, a small town on the south coast of Saxon England, by St Wilfrid. Wilfrid successfully converted pagan Saxons on the southern coast of England to Christianity. Historians tell us that St Wilfrid was successful in recruiting pagans partly because he taught Saxons how to fish more effectively. One might say that the best Christians are skilled Christians.

Selchester Cathedral was moved ten miles northwards and inland from Sealsey four hundred years later to the city of Selchester. Perhaps the Saxon Britons had climate change models which predicted rapid sea-level rises. If so these climate models were as faulty as our current models since Sealsey is still on the coast and above water thirteen centuries later. More likely the move inland was prompted by political considerations. Religion and politics were interwoven in those days. Sealsey continued to thrive above the waves, while Selchester grew into a cathedral city of some importance to Norman England.

The infectious high-pitched laughter from over his right shoulder warned Joseph that one of his closest friends, Dr Neil Watson, was close.

"Joseph, you old dog, you must be proud of your achievement at such an advanced age," joked Neil. "You have been ordained in the nick of time before your senile dementia carries you to our maker."

Father Sage had been teased frequently about his age at the college. He was a comfortable ten years older than the next-oldest student. Indeed, he was older than many of his tutors. Joseph Sage, as he was known as a student, had spent several years working as a police constable in northern England before he had finally taken the plunge to train for the priesthood. He had become disillusioned with excessive bureaucracy, cuts to frontline staff, and politically correct limitation on effective police techniques such as stop-and-search policies, which had triggered riots in his area. The chair of the local police committee at that time had praised rioters and had even stated that they would have been "apathetic fools if they did not protest."

The rioters, thus enthused by police leaders, had organised riots which had destroyed many buildings and injured over a thousand police officers. Police reinforcements had been drafted from every region of the country. CS gas grenades and water cannons did not succeed in stemming the violence. Community policing became impossible in certain parts of the city in groups of fewer than twenty officers for safety. In light of what he perceived as anarchy, Constable Joseph Sage had taken the plunge and applied to Selchester College to train as a priest. At his age, it was not easy to resume full-time education. Joseph had struggled with the self-discipline of adult learning. However, with support from teachers and from friends like Dr Watson, Joseph had passed his final examinations, and Father Sage had emerged like a religious butterfly, hoping to pollinate the world of unbelievers with Christian faith.

"Now, don't let your fixed ideas about tradition prevent you from connecting with all of your flock, Father," Dr Watson admonished to Joseph.

It had been a running joke that Joseph was not comfortable with the rapid pace of change within his branch of the Christian church. If Joseph had been given the choice, mass would still be in Latin, priests would all be male, homosexual relationships would still be a criminal offence—or even a medical disorder requiring treatment—and baptism or marriages would only be offered to those who demonstrated their faith by attending church on a regular basis for a sustained period of years. For Joseph, the life of a Christian was the outwards demonstration of faith. Many of his fellow ordinands that day, on the other hand, were much more sanguine about any and all of the modern changes within the church and society, as well as the huge variation in practices within the church. Gay relationships, women priests, happy clappy services, relaxed recruitment criteria—all these were just fine by the majority of newly ordained priests. Now Father Sage and his colleagues would each be free to pursue their own kind of churchmanship in the real world.

"Very funny, Neil. As my favourite pop group tell us, 'all you need is love,' and all will be well," responded Father Sage to Dr Watson.

Another ordinand with whom Joseph was friendly, Father Jesus O'Sullivan, joined them and offered congratulations. The two priests and the doctor shared a few more teasing comments before they were interrupted by the slow, dry drawl of a familiar and unwelcome voice.

"Well, well. I am surprised—but delighted, of course—to find such a variegated band of brothers at the ordination today." Father Leonard Gibot fired his opening salvo at the two friends as he mingled with the other graduates.

Leonard Gibot was one of the intellectual stars of Selchester College. He had achieved top grades in every exam and had been noticed by senior church academics and leaders. It was a poorly kept secret that he had been marked for rapid advancement within the church. On the liberal wing of the church, he embraced any and all of the changes which were proposed by the General Synod. Nothing was too radical or too liberal for him. He was able to trace his ancestry back to Norman times when the minor

Norman aristocratic Gibot family had followed Duke William on a conquest of Britain. This family history counted for nothing in his mind compared to his personal ambition. Some of his fellow students had felt that he had sacrificed much of his sincerity on the altar of populism. However, none could doubt his talent for political manoeuvring and for attracting positive attention from the most senior church leaders.

"I really am surprised at your academic achievement, Father Sage," whined Father Gibot. "Seeing you ordained is one of life's mysteries, indeed. Your early academic challenges were one thing, and your rather crude sociopolitical views seemed to me to suggest that you were suited to another calling. In particular, I will never forget your defense of anachronistic myths such as the literal virgin birth and resurrection. You are a source of endless astonishment to my friends and me. Precisely what place there is for you in the modern Anglican communion is beyond me. Then again, thinking was never your strong suit, was it, Joseph?"

Without waiting for a reply, Father Gibot now turned his scornful gaze on the other graduate in the group.

"And Father O'Sullivan has also surprised us all with his persistence," Gibot said, lowering his voice to a whisper. "Another seed which fell on stony ground only to germinate into a weed of remarkable tenacity. How you manage to sustain yourself on a diet of cat and dog food is amazing to those of us in the white race. Is there really a post in Britain for people of your tribe? Or perhaps our little chocolate brothers in faith in the Caribbean will find a position for you to preach to your own kind? I really don't know what the world is coming to. Coons, niggers, wogs, and every other species or vermin is being allowed into civilised society these days," Father Gibot taunted in a vicious whisper to Father O'Sullivan.

Father Sage looked at his friend and thought to himself, *this hypocritical, power hungry, racist fool pretends to be so liberal and tolerant. Why do we let him get away with this?*

Father O'Sullivan was unique amongst the pale white ordinands at Selchester. His most obviously unique feature in this group of pale white men was that his skin was as black as the ace of spades. His ancestors had been sold into slavery by their equally black-skinned rulers in Africa and then transported to Jamaica to work in the sugarcane fields in the seventeenth century. These ancestors had bequeathed Father O'Sullivan the skin of a deep ebony hue. This stood out in stark contrast to the bright white and pink of all other ordinands on this day of Caribbean sunshine in England.

Father Sage and O'Sullivan were already aware of the overt disdain from Father Gibot. They each grimaced at the crude and deliberate racist provocation. They managed to contain their disgust and refused to be drawn into a public altercation with their acerbic colleague on such a day of celebration.

"What is that foul stench?" Joseph Sage said to Dr Watson and Father O'Sullivan. "There is something really rotten nearby."

Father Gibot smiled with thin compressed lips, satisfied with the insults he had sprayed this morning. He nodded slowly to his two fellow ordinands and walked past both of them towards the purple cassock of a bishop several feet away.

"Ah, Father Gibot," crowed the bishop. "Let me introduce you to the archbishop…"

Father Sage, Dr Watson, and O'Sullivan raised eyebrows to each other in a signal of mutual support, resignation, and disgust.

"I believe my favourite singer-songwriter once suggested cursing Sir Walter Raleigh because he was 'such a stupid get.' Perhaps we should curse Father Gibot for the same reason…" suggested Father Sage.

"Now, now, Joseph. 'Let it be' might be an appropriate policy for the current situation. Leonard

Gibot is entitled to free speech even if it makes us nauseous," responded Father O'Sullivan soothingly. He and Joseph shook hands and bade each other farewell.

Over the course of three years at Selchester College, Joseph Sage had developed an enthusiastic dislike of Leonard Gibot. This was made easier by the casual and spiteful racism which Leonard Gibot so easily spat towards anyone whom he considered of impure or inferior race. How could anyone pretend to hold such liberal views for public consumption while actually fomenting such bigotry and hatred in private? Joseph had discussed this often with friends over a beer in a local hostelry. It had tested his ability to love his enemy on many occasions.

Three hours later, ceremonials complete and all congratulations exchanged, Joseph Sage and Dr Watson walked across the manicured grass of the college green to the college refectory. They had been friends since senior school days. They were still mildly annoyed by the frosty exchange with Father Gibot.

"Which of your Ten Commandments covers that conversation with Father Gibot?" asked Dr Watson about the earlier encounter. "Are you forbidden from giving false witness against Father Gibot or just forbidden from murdering him?"

"I think that the more important instruction is the one to forgive our enemy," countered Father Sage. "In many ways Father Gibot is a product of his social context and has little insight into his twisted views. I don't really blame him entirely for his racism. I pity him, and I will pray for him. Just as I pray for you, Neil. You need salvation just as much as Father Gibot, albeit for different reasons. Indeed, we all need forgiveness and salvation for our many sins and weaknesses."

"Well, I am not as forgiving as you," replied Dr Watson. "I don't have the same supernatural beliefs as you. I think Father Gibot is a racist and bigot and needs to be confronted with his hateful views. Unless we speak up against this nonsense, it will continue and spread, and our culture and society will be degraded."

After a pot of tea and sandwiches, the time arrived for the two friends to part. They embraced and bade each other a temporary farewell. Father Sage was travelling to a coastal city in the north of England to his first post as an Anglican chaplain attached to a cathedral and a large university, while Dr Watson was working as a junior doctor in the same city and close to the chapel where Father Sage was starting his new career.

"Best of luck in your chaplaincy up north, you old goat. I will no doubt see you often up there," said Dr Watson. "Watch out for Gibot. He will rise fast in the church, and if he can put his size-nine boots on your neck to get higher, he will."

"And all the best to you in your hospital career. We will need to meet up regularly so that I can keep an eye on your spiritual well-being," replied Father Sage.

Neither Joseph nor Jesus was under any illusion about Leonard Gibot. It is probably just as well neither of them knew just how tragic future events would prove to be.

CHAPTER 2

THE BURSAR

The year after his ordination, Father Leonard Gibot approached the bursar's door quietly and gave it a gentle tap. The bursar of Selchester College of Theology, Arthur Peterson, had a large and comfortable office on the college campus, as befitting a man who controlled all of college finances.

"Please enter," boomed the bursar from behind his desk.

"Ah, Bursar, good morning to you. Do you have a moment?" asked Father Gibot. "I have some thoughts I need to discuss." Leonard opened the door and smiled warmly.

"Certainly, Leonard," responded Arthur Peterson. "Please take a seat."

Leonard slid into a comfortable leather armchair opposite the bursar's desk. There was a pause as the bursar finished reading from a ledger, snapped it shut, and moved it to the edge of his desk. He took off his spectacles and leaned back in his chair.

"Now how can I help this morning?" the bursar asked.

"I wanted to raise the issue of my academic fees," Leonard said.

"Of course, Leonard," he replied. "Very happy to advise about this. What was it that you needed to know?"

"As you may know, I graduated last year. Since then it has been a struggle for me to find the full payment for my fees to cover my final academic year. I have looked at various options in terms of optimising income. I wondered whether you might be in a position to help with some of these?"

"Well, there is not usually much we can do," answered the bursar. "I can sometimes ask the college principal to postpone fee payment for a short period. However, this is only a temporary solution and cannot be repeated very often. I normally advise our old students to approach their bank for a loan. Some banks are very helpful for new priests struggling with living costs."

"Yes, thank you, Bursar. I did try this last year, and my bank was helpful, but I fear that my creditworthiness will not permit a repeat performance this year," replied Leonard with a slight frown. "I was hoping that you might be able to help from a different perspective…a personal perspective, if you catch my drift."

There was a lengthy pause, and Arthur Peterson stared at Leonard Gibot's face, searching for meaning.

"A personal perspective? What exactly does that mean?" asked the bursar.

"Well, I thought you might be willing to help me out yourself without needing to inform the college formally," replied Father Gibot.

"I don't think this would be appropriate, Father Gibot. My position at the college does not permit me to lend money to alumni. No, I don't think we should even be discussing such a suggestion. This would be a conflict of interest at the very least," protested the bursar.

"Yes, I can see your point, of course," responded Father Gibot. "I entirely agree. Please forget I ever suggested it. On another matter entirely, since I am here today, I wanted to mention that I have come across some information. Some information that might be very interesting to the wrong sort of nosy journalist. I bring this up only to reassure you of my utmost discretion." Leonard let this statement hang between the two men for several seconds.

"I am so sorry. I still don't really understand what you are getting at," Arthur said.

"This is a sensitive matter, Bursar. I fully understand your reticence, of course. The information I have received is from the children's home. It is quite persuasive and could be very embarrassing. I am only saying that you have absolutely nothing to worry about from my perspective. My total discretion is, of course, absolutely guaranteed," replied Father Gibot.

Arthur Peterson swallowed hard and loosened his collar. A series of disastrous but inevitable events unfolded in his mind as he contemplated the information that Leonard had discovered falling into the public domain.

Several months later, the telephone rang on the desk of Arthur Peterson. Arthur looked up from his copy of the *Daily Telegraph* and glanced at the wall clock. *It is 8:30 a.m., and the phone rings. Very unusual*, he thought. *Must be important or a wrong number.*

"Selchester 4600. Arthur Peterson, bursar, speaking," he announced into the telephone receiver.

"Good morning, Bursar. This is the porters' lodge, sir. My apologies for bothering you so early, but there are two policemen in the lodge who want a word with you, sir," the porter explained.

"Yes, of course. Show them up to my office, please," Arthur said.

Ten minutes later, two policemen in plain clothes were ushered into the large, oak-trimmed bursar's office.

After both policemen sat opposite the bursar's desk, one of the policemen spoke. "Thank you for seeing us, Mr Peterson. I am Detective Inspector Morley, and this is Detective Sergeant Ryan. We are here about a serious matter, and we thought it best to meet you as early as possible."

"Of course, gentlemen. I will help you in any way I can," Arthur replied.

"Mr Peterson, it has come to our attention that there are some irregularities in the accounts over the past three months," started DI Morley. "We are aware that more than £20,000 has gone missing from the college's current account. We wondered if you were aware of this."

Arthur sat still for a few seconds as small beads of sweat appeared over his forehead and temples. He swallowed hard. "I was not aware of this issue at all. That is, I—I am sure there must be some mistake. Perhaps you could give me some details, and I will certainly look into this immediately," stammered Mr Peterson.

"Perhaps it might be more advisable if you were to accompany us to the station to discuss the details," suggested DI Morley.

"I don't think that is really necessary," replied Mr Peterson. "I have all of the college accounts to hand on the premises. I can answer any questions better from these offices if you could just clarify the nature of your enquiry."

"Well, the truth is, we already have considerable financial details, Mr Peterson," DI Morley said. "We have already seen the recent accounts and bank statements, provided by your banks, which confirm that the alleged transactions did occur. What we are now seeking is an explanation. You see, we have examined the college accounts closely, and there is indeed a large amount of money missing. It has been paid out over several months in instalments to an account in the name of A. Peterson. We have also confirmed with your bank that the money arrived in your account. There may, of course, be an entirely innocent explanation for this matter. So...perhaps you could just explain what lies behind this."

Arthur Peterson sighed and looked at the ceiling. He swallowed hard again and opened his mouth to speak, but no words came out. He swallowed again, and when he spoke, it came as a whisper. "I accept what you say. You are absolutely correct. The fault is mine, of course. I cannot justify what has been done. I will resign, of course, with immediate effect, and I will repay any funds accidentally paid to the wrong account."

The two detectives glanced at each other, and Detective Inspector Morley spoke. "Arthur Peterson, I am arresting you on suspicion of embezzlement. You do not have to say anything. But it may harm your defense if you do not mention, when questioned, something that you later rely on in court. Anything you do say may be given in evidence."

The postmortem examination on Arthur Peterson confirmed death by strangulation. There were no suspicious circumstances, and the coroner recorded a verdict of suicide.

Arthur Peterson's widow and son, George, were devastated by his sudden suicide. The college tried to help as far as possible in such tragic circumstances. George's education was supplemented by occasional grants from the college hardship fund. In due course, George was offered a post of deacon at the Cathedral of Christ the King in northern England.

CHAPTER 3

THE ACCIDENT

Global social media platform suppresses free press by suspending researcher for revealing collusion between journalists and far-left Antifa movement.
—*Breitbart News,* 2018

M any years later, the country lane in northern England was particularly peaceful and beautiful at this time of year. The summer leaves were a rich green. It was midmorning, and the only sound was the beautiful English summer birdsong.

Amy Lambert walked to work along a beautiful English country lane, enjoying the less-than-a-mile walk from her university to the farm shop where she cashiered. She enjoyed the work, which was undemanding. Her colleagues who worked the farm were friendly and kind. Amy was saving to pay her tuition fees at university. This particular morning, Amy was calculating in her head how many more days she would need to work over the summer break to cover her living costs during her first term in the coming academic year.

Amy was only distantly aware of the sound of a car engine approaching from behind. The car hit her at a speed close to ninety miles per hour. The car bumper fractured both of her legs in multiple places. Her head hit the bonnet of the car, and her skull fractured. Bone fragments from her skull passed into her cerebral cortex, causing massive neurological trauma. Her body slipped under the car as it decelerated. The link between her vertebral column and her skull was severed as her neck passed under the front wheel of the car.

Amy was killed virtually instantly by the impact. The coroner's inquest recorded that it was an accidental death.

Bishop Leonard Gibot awoke in a hospital bed.

He had risen the ranks swiftly as he had intended and had been granted a bishopric within a few years of ordination. This was a rare honour amongst Anglican clergy. He had been promoted to a bishopric in northern England at a comparatively young age partly because his flexibility to align with the morals and principles of the modern world had been noticed by the highest church authorities. In this climate, rigid adherence to orthodox Christian beliefs was not an asset. Firm moral principles based on Christian heritage and culture were seen as a thing of the past. He was seen as a person with a very bright future at the highest level.

He was unsure where he was and how he had arrived in a hospital bed. *I am clearly in a hospital judging by the tube in my nose and the tubes attached to my arms,* he thought. *This all suggests that my situation might be serious.* This occurred to him as his level of awareness gradually sharpened. He became aware of pain in the centre of his face, his right shoulder, and the centre of his chest. He looked around his bed. He seemed to be in a small hospital ward with only a handful of other patients, all of whom were hooked up to multiple beeping and flashing machines. *What in heaven's name has happened?* he thought to himself. He tried to raise his right arm, but this was too painful. He raised his left arm instead in a gesture to a nurse holding a chart at the foot of another patient's bed. The nurse approached him.

"Where am I, and what happened?" he asked the nurse in a hoarse whisper.

"You were in a car accident. You have been in hospital for several weeks. You had a serious head injury, and you have been unconscious since you arrived. You broke some bones, but you are recovering," said the nurse reassuringly.

The bishop felt thirsty and hungry, and he could feel the stiffness in his muscles and joints from lying in bed for so long.

"Am I likely to need more treatment, and will I need to stay here for long?" he asked the nurse.

"You will need physiotherapy, and you will need to use a sling for a few weeks. Now that you are awake, we will help you sit out of bed, and you should start walking within days. With a fair wind, you should be home in a few weeks," said the nurse. "I will get a doctor who can explain in more detail."

One week later, the bishop was sitting out of his hospital bed following his physiotherapist's advice and exercising his shoulder. One of the junior nurses entered the small ward accompanied by a smart young man in a suit and tie.

"Bishop Gibot, this is Detective Inspector Malcolm Everton. He has asked to see you to go through some details of the accident," said the nurse.

"Oh, yes, of course. I would be happy to talk to you, Detective Inspector. Please pull up a chair," replied the bishop, smiling warmly.

Malcolm pulled up a plastic chair and sat facing the bishop.

"Thank you, Your Grace," opened Malcolm. "I have some details of the road accident from the traffic police report. However, I wanted to understand the circumstances leading up the accident in a little more detail."

"Of course, Inspector. I will help if I can. However, I have no recollection of the accident whatsoever. Indeed, I cannot remember most of the week preceding the accident. The doctors have been through this many times with me, and the details are just missing. I understand this is quite common after a blow to the head."

"Yes, of course. I fully understand," Malcolm said. "But just in case, I wondered if you had any idea what you were doing before the accident and where you were going to?"

"No, sorry. It is a complete blank, Inspector," replied the bishop.

"And I also wondered if you could remember where you had been and whether you had consumed any alcohol before the accident?" Malcolm said with slightly raised eyebrows.

The bishop shook his head. "No again. I am so sorry, Inspector, but I simply cannot help you," replied the bishop.

"Well, thank you for seeing me anyway," Malcolm said. "If you remember anything else, please don't hesitate to contact me. This card has my contact details on it."

The policeman placed a card on the bedside table, rose, and shook the bishop's good hand before walking out of the hospital ward. On his way past the nurses' station, he caught the eye of the duty nurse and offered sight of his professional ID.

"Hello there. I am Detective Inspector Everton. I was wondering if the results of the blood tests taken from Bishop Gibot had come back yet. I have been informed that the blood was tested for alcohol, and we need to confirm that the alcohol level was negligible as a matter of routine after a fatal road traffic accident. Are you able to take a peek for these results for me, please?"

"I am so sorry, Inspector," replied the nurse. "There has been a technical difficulty at the lab. All of the blood taken from the bishop on admission to the hospital has been lost. This happens rarely, but when it does we need to take replacement samples. In the bishop's case, repeat samples were sent but not until three days after admission to hospital. The bishop was in a coma for this period, as you know. As a result, it is not possible to establish the blood alcohol level on admission to the hospital."

Malcolm scratched his head. "I see. Well, we can't do anything about this, I suppose," he said. "We will just have to accept it. We will never know for sure."

He left the hospital and drove to the scene of the accident. The country lane where Amy Lambert had died was deserted at this time of the afternoon in rural northern England. He had the report from the traffic officer, which documented that the distance from the impact to the place where the car and the body had been found was just less than eighty feet. From this the officer at the scene had calculated that the speed of the car at the time of impact had been approximately thirty miles per hour. The speed limit on this country lane was sixty miles per hour.

Malcolm was still able to see the marks from the impact. He looked at the black stain on the tarmac. *What a sad reminder that human bodies are essentially a bag of fluid which can so easily be punctured*, he thought to himself.

He walked along the road, following the black stain from the tyres as the bishop had tried to brake. These brake marks did not start until just after the marks from Amy Lambert's body hitting the road surface. As he paced the distance of the brake marks, he counted up the distance. After a few minutes, he came to the place where the car had stopped and the tyre marks ceased.

This car had taken almost four hundred feet to stop, thought DI Everton. *That is way more than the official report.* He did a quick calculation in his head. *That gives us a speed in excess of eighty miles per hour for the car at impact. There is something odd here. My calculations should not be so different from the official estimates, surely?*

Gerard Harrison, a local journalist, was meeting the grieving Lambert family. Charles Lambert, Amy's brother, and her mother, Dorothy, were meeting Gerard at the offices of *The Daily Post*, the local newspaper for which Mr Harrison worked. Mr Harrison invited them both to sit in his small, rather untidy office on the seventh floor of the *Post* building. The office block stood on the banks of the river looking out into the estuary and the Irish sea.

"Thank you for meeting us, Mr Harrison," opened Charles Lambert. "My mother and I wanted to ask for your help to investigate the recent death of our sister, Amy."

"This is not a problem, Mr Lambert. I will help in any way I can. What can I do?" responded Mr Harrison.

Mrs Lambert did not speak but sat dabbing her eyes and listening to the two men.

"Amy was killed last month in the road accident," explained Charles. "Amy was walking to work on the day she died. Initially we were told by the police that it appeared that the driver had been exceeding the speed limit. Subsequently, the police changed their view and informed us that the calculations from the scene of the accident suggested that the car was travelling within the speed limit. It is a matter of public knowledge that the driver of the car was Bishop Leonard Gibot. There are rumours that the bishop struggles with alcohol dependence. The coroner's inquest was concluded very rapidly and simply concluded that Amy Lambert had suffered an accidental death. We are very suspicious that there has been a cover-up. We are not sure how to investigate this further, and we wondered if you might use your skills to uncover the truth."

"I have heard some rumours about Bishop Gibot," replied Mr Harrison. "I will certainly make some enquiries on your behalf. It would be worth starting with the police, and I have some solid contacts in our local force. Leave it with me for a few days, and I will let you know what I can uncover."

The Lamberts shook Mr Harrison's hand and left him in hope that some of the truth would be uncovered.

Gerard Harrison had an ongoing professional friendship with several policemen in the north of England. One of these was the investigating officer, Detective Inspector Malcolm Everton. Gerard had no difficulty arranging a meeting with DI Everton at The Pen and Wig, a small pub in the centre of the city's business district. The pub was a favourite for local solicitors, policemen, and journalists. It was particularly noted for the discreet booths which allowed private conversations. It was rumoured that most of the leaks from the law enforcement services and legal profession which appeared on the pages of *The Daily Post* occurred over a half pint of local ale at The Pen and Wig.

Gerard carried two foaming pints of ale to the small table at which DI Everton sat.

"Hello, Malcolm. Thank you for meeting me," opened Gerard.

"No problem, Gerard. Happy to help out if I can," replied Malcolm.

"OK. Cheers." Both men took a sip of their beer. "I have been approached by the family of Amy Lambert, the girl who was killed in the recent road accident. They think there has been some sort of cover-up to protect Bishop Gibot. Can you shed any light?" asked Gerard.

Malcolm paused and looked around the saloon bar of the pub. It was midmorning, and there were very few patrons in at this time.

"This is a tricky one, Gerard," said Malcolm. "I cannot reveal details of an ongoing investigation, of course. However—strictly off the record, of course— I have come up against some obstacles that are hard to grapple with. The records from the traffic police suggest that the car was travelling very slowly, probably much less than the speed limit for that road. I visited the scene of the accident to have a look first-hand, and my calculations suggest that the speed of impact was way above the speed limit. Of course, the official traffic report was submitted to the coroner, and my rough calculations have no official status. Then the hospital blood tests on Bishop Gibot have conveniently gone missing, and it is impossible to establish a blood alcohol level at the time of the accident. Ultimately, the coroner concluded this was an accidental death based on the evidence submitted by the police forensic experts. I did raise some informal concerns with those on the top floor at police HQ. I was told to stick to the official line and to avoid any risk of allegations that we were targeting the bishop. Religious discrimination, blah blah blah. You know, the normal politically correct nonsense from the higher-ups."

"I see. So there is no way to get to the real truth in this matter," replied Gerard. "Is there any way I can publish any of this?"

"I don't think so," said Malcolm. "It is all supposition and guesswork. No objective evidence. Unless the forensic chaps who give the official speed calculations change their tune, we have to accept their expert view. And unless the bishop's blood tests magically reappear, there is nothing to prove any wrongdoing. The bishop is looking untouchable, despite what you and I might suspect."

Three weeks later, Bishop Gibot was sitting at home, struggling to pour his milk in his tea due to the infernal sling on his arm. The doctors had advised him to wear the sling to help his broken collarbone heal. *What an inconvenience*, he thought.

Deputy Assistant Commissioner of Police Jeremy Thatcher sat opposite him, sipping from his cup of tea.

"Leonard, it has been very difficult to arrange things in a satisfactory manner this time. It has taken all of my resources with our friends in the chapter to make matters agreeable. I had to use a considerable number of my contacts to ensure that your blood samples disappeared to avoid any alcohol testing. It has also been very difficult to square things with the coroner and to ensure that the report from the traffic police did not find evidence of excessive speed. I am not sure if we can continue to solve problems in this way. There are limits to the influence of our organisation," said the policeman.

"Yes, yes, yes, I fully appreciate all of your help as always, Jeremy. After my last little problem, I really hoped to keep my drinking under severe control. I don't really know what happened this time, but I promise I will stay clear of the hard stuff."

"The family of the young girl, Amy Lambert, who was killed, are still making noises," replied the commissioner. "They have been very unwilling to accept a simple finding of accidental death. They have been making enquiries about your past record, and it has been very hard to conceal everything effectively. Also, the local press are snooping around asking very inconvenient questions. It is important for you to keep your head down for a while, Leonard. To this end, I suggest a period of rest and recuperation at this rehabilitation hospital."

Deputy Commissioner Thatcher passed a card to Bishop Gibot. "I have made arrangements for your transfer. This will keep you out of the public eye for a period. You have several injuries which make this plausible. It will also help with the confidential detoxification side of things. Are you willing to do this for me?" asked the policeman.

"Yes, all right. If I must, I will attend and keep my head down for a few more weeks. These blasted medics make our lives so difficult," replied Bishop Gibot.

The private rehab hospital was set in beautiful gardens in rural England. Leonard Gibot could not fault the view over the rolling English countryside. The trouble was the place was so boring. And to cap it all off, there was no booze, and he had to eat those blasted Antabuse tablets which made him feel decidedly off.

"Here you are, Leonard. These are the cakes you asked for." The nurse placed a carrier bag of groceries on Leonard's bedside table.

"Thank you so much, Michael. Here, take this for your trouble." Leonard pressed two twenty-pound notes into Michael's hand.

As soon as Michael was out of the room, Leonard reached below the bag of pastries and took the bottle of Inchgower single-malt whisky from the grocery bag. He poured a generous two fingers into his teacup and then folded the bottle into his dressing gown before placing it at the back of the lowest drawer of this chest of drawers.

As Leonard swallowed the whisky, he felt the delightful burning at the back of his throat and in his stomach. *Two months without a drop*, he thought. *Absolute hell.* A healthy life, perhaps, but hardly a life worth living. He sat staring from his hospital window for a few minutes before downing the remaining whisky in one swig.

Fifteen minutes later, he started to feel rather hot. He noticed he was sweating even though he was sitting still. A dull ache began in his left shoulder and then spread to his left arm and into his chest. He wanted to speak or shout for help but found he could not move his mouth at all. With a great effort, he managed to move his right hand to the emergency call button and press it.

When the duty nurse arrived in Leonard's room, he had fallen from his seat. He was breathing but unconscious. His lips were turning blue.

The crash team was summoned and arrived four minutes later. An IV line was already in place. The ECG had already confirmed that Leonard had probably suffered a heart attack. The blood tests proved this to be accurate over the following two days.

The doctors informed Bishop Gibot that he was very lucky to have survived. They knew he had been drinking again and told him that the alcohol had reacted adversely with his medication, contributing to the heart attack. They also warned him that he would probably not survive another heart attack.

Several weeks after his discharge from hospital, Bishop Gibot was at home opening his mail. He liked to open his own mail as a general rule.

Throughout the morning, he was working through a small pile of official correspondence in his living room in his pyjamas. He sliced open a white envelope with his silver gilt paper slicer, sending a single piece of paper toppling onto his desk surface. He noticed that the letter was typed in block capitals and unsigned. The letter contained a clear message.

"We know what you are and what you have done. You are a murderer. You must resign your position immediately. Unless you repent, you will be punished and exposed. We will not be silenced."

The bishop reread the message carefully several times. It was not clear which alleged crime this message referred to. He poised the document over the cross-cut shredder next to his desk. To ignore or not to ignore? This was only the latest threatening letter in a series which stretched back several years. He decided not to destroy this one. He folded it, placed it carefully back inside the envelope, and tucked it into his pyjama breast pocket.

He lifted the telephone from his desk and dialled. "Hello, Jeremy. Leonard here. I have a small problem. I wonder if you can help me. I have received another of these letters. I have it here with me now. Any chance you might pop over to pick it up and find the culprit?" asked the bishop.

CHAPTER 4

EXORCISM

Father Sage approached the wide double doors of the Irish Centre. The Victorian sandstone building was only a single storey but had been built at a time when such a single-storey building was over twenty feet high. The building was situated immediately next to the cathedral at the foot of the large and imposing stairs leading to the cathedral's main entrance. The original architect had encrusted the exterior with references to Irish life, including harp emblems and shamrocks. The bright autumn sunshine complemented the warm red sandstone of the facade. A century earlier, it would have been an attractive and thriving hub for the large Irish community in this coastal city. Sadly, over the century since it had been built, neglect and decay had taken their toll. Buddleia plants and various grasses were thriving in the gutters and between roof tiles, prising the bricks, stones, and tiles apart, slowly dismembering a once-proud building. This was a slow and rather ugly degenerative death for the building. Health and Safety notices outside the door and on the walls proclaimed the risks to all who passed by and warned of dire consequences of entering without great care and complex protective equipment.

Several weeks earlier, Father Sage had met Gregory Mannheim, a professor of Irish studies, at the small cathedral refectory within a stone's throw of the Irish Centre. The meeting had been requested by Professor Mannheim without much detail or context. Father Sage expected the usual mixture of social and religious concerns, including a life event of a negative nature, which often triggered a request for a private meeting with a priest.

"Good morning, Father. I am so pleased you could meet me." Professor Mannheim shook Father Sage's hand warmly. There was just a trace of a soft Southern Irish accent from the professor.

"My pleasure, Professor. Let me buy the coffee, or would you prefer tea this morning?" replied Father Sage.

With warm drinks paid for, the two men found a convenient, slightly secluded table, out of sight from the passing street.

"I appreciate you meeting me, Father. I have a rather strange story to tell you and then a request which you might find even stranger," Professor Mannheim confided in hushed tones.

Father Sage knew how to listen. A nod of his head was all that was needed to give Professor Mannheim permission to tell his tale.

"It all began a couple of years ago. My role at the university involves organising and fundraising for the Irish Society. I was aware that their original premises, the Irish Centre, is not in a great state of repair. As I discovered more, it appeared that my predecessors had struggled over many years to use the Irish Centre. Every time an attempt was made to refurbish or repair it, something happened to put problems in the way. Usually something dangerous or frankly harmful happened. Several people have been killed and several others seriously injured over the past few years. It is almost as if someone has been trying to prevent the building from being refurbished or occupied. My immediate predecessor as professor of Irish studies disappeared for two months before his body was found. He had been dead inside the Irish Centre for two months when they found his body. The official story was a heart attack..."

Professor Mannheim paused, looked away and out of the window, then looked back at Father Sage for reassurance that this story was not too ridiculous.

"Please go on, Professor." Father Sage nodded assent for the tale to continue.

"It wasn't a heart attack, Father. I am convinced of this. Heart attacks do not decapitate middle-aged professors of Irish studies. He was found without his head. It had been twisted off his body. Are you aware of the forces required to twist a head from a human body? Such forces require superhuman strength. Also, there was little sign of bleeding on or near the body. It was as if the blood had clotted before death. Someone, or something, with inhuman strength committed this murder. I managed to obtain the original reports of the murder from contacts in the Irish community within the police. The official story remained a heart attack and then a fall against a sharp mechanical object. This is entirely implausible in my view. In my opinion, there was a cover-up, and I have no idea why."

Professor Mannheim paused long enough to drink some coffee and used the opportunity to look carefully around the small refectory. Father Sage noticed something more than caution—more like suspicion and even some fear—in the professor's eyes.

"I became concerned and started to look back in the records. That's when I found the tales of successive attempts to repair the Irish Centre over many decades. In most cases, these were abandoned after a death or serious injury in similar suspicious and gruesome circumstances. I have visited the Irish Centre several times. At first glance it appears just like any other dilapidated old Victorian building. However, once inside, things happen which I cannot explain. I hear noises and see things in the corner of my eyes which confuse me. It feels as if someone is talking to me in a very faint voice and in a foreign language which I cannot quite understand."

Professor Mannheim paused and looked around the refectory again.

"I am not sure why you are telling me this, Professor," Father Sage said. "Would it not be more appropriate to talk to the police again? In what way can I help you?"

Professor Mannheim stared at Father Sage intently as if debating whether to go on.

"Father, I think the Irish Centre is haunted, or possessed, if a building can be possessed. I think that something evil is in there. I wondered whether you could exorcise the Centre and remove the evil before someone else is harmed?"

"Professor, I honestly don't think it is likely that an exorcism will help. Old buildings are dangerous places and should only be visited with health and safety precautions. Surely you need health and safety experts," replied Father Sage.

"I've already been down that route, and it got me nowhere," replied the Professor. "The local Health and Safety Executive inspector ran away after we visited the property together. It was he who suggested demolition or an exorcism…"

Father Sage said, "I should perhaps explain to you my understanding of exorcism, Professor Mannheim. There is a distinct difference between religion and God. Religion is man's way of celebrating and recognising God or asking for help. God is more powerful than any of us can imagine. God can do anything. There is no limit to his power, but we cannot invoke God's power at will. There are many religious ceremonies such as exorcism which are the way men ask for help from God. The ceremony does not in itself achieve anything. We can ask God for help, but only God knows if help is needed or deserved. Exorcism is not like a simple switch that removes or dismisses an evil entity. So, you see, I have my doubts that exorcism would be of any use when you have an old, dilapidated building which is intrinsically unsafe. At the end of an exorcism you will probably still have an unsafe building. It sounds as if demolition and rebuilding is the right choice."

"I appreciate your perspective, Father," replied Professor Mannheim. "But I am convinced that a spiritual remedy is needed for a problem which appears of a supernatural nature."

Father Sage tried a more detailed explanation to convince the professor that he should seek a secular solution. "Let me explain in more detail, Professor. Exorcism was a relatively common event in seventeenth-century England when demonic possession was a real feature of life to many common folk. However, demonic possession has not been considered a valid and rational concept by modern scientists for several hundred years. Demons—which disobey the laws of physics, biology, and chemistry—are no longer considered anything more than a fantasy for novels and Hollywood by the overwhelming majority of people. Systematic classification of medical disorders began over four hundred years ago and has effectively excluded supernatural forces as an explanation of medical conditions.

"Symptoms previously attributed to demonic possession such as ecstasy, seizures, insanity, and an agitated state of mind have been attributed to a variety of well-understood medical conditions by modern medical science. The church supports these modern medical attitudes to alleged demonic possession in most cases. More complex and puzzling phenomena such as secret knowledge, being able to predict the future accurately, knowledge of complex things that one has never learned, knowledge of languages one has never learned, and supernatural strength are also often explained with reference to mental and neurological disorders, for example Schizophrenia and other psychotic disorders, by contemporary scientists and medical doctors.

"The signs of alleged demonic possession have always been rather nonspecific. These include examples like horrible shouting, jeering at one's neighbour, deformation of movements, removing clothes, self-lacerating, inhuman revelry, torment of bodies, unusual injuries of the body and of those nearby, extraordinary motion of bodies such as running as fast as a horse, forgetfulness of things done, melancholy, and the acceleration of death. Some of these so-called diagnostic signs seem a little ambiguous and general to contemporary secular sceptics."

Father Sage paused to allow Professor Mannheim an opportunity to accept this rather secular view of the world. The professor appeared rather unconvinced.

Father Sage continued. "Modern medicine has even formulated a convenient 'disorder,' which is neatly called demonopathy, in which the patient believes that he or she is possessed by one or more demons. The implication is that this is merely a disorder of perception or delusion and not a reality. Sceptics might agree with this rational explanation. The fact that exorcism relieves the symptoms for some people who perceive symptoms of demonic possession is often attributed to the placebo effect and the power of psychological suggestion. No doubt both the placebo effect and psychological suggestion are very powerful forces in the hands of experts and to the minds of the vulnerable. This does seem a more plausible explanation than supernatural forces."

"I can assure you, I am not suffering from demonopathy, Father Sage," replied the professor. "However, organised religions all have belief in some form of supernatural force, so the expulsion of supernatural powers by a supernatural ceremony would seem consistent with religious belief. My opinion in this matter is certainly no more incredible than your belief in the resurrection of Christ," countered Professor Mannheim.

"There can be no doubt that the Christian belief about demonic possession is a genuine phenomenon in the minds of some sincere Christians," accepted Father Sage. "Whether some of those professing such a belief, and supporting exorcism as a process, are right or not is another matter entirely."

Father Sage and Professor Mannheim discussed the pros and cons backwards and forwards for half an hour. Eventually, Father Sage agreed to raise the matter with his bishop, and then with higher authorities within the church, to satisfy the professor.

A few days later, Father Sage and Bishop Gibot talked over what was possible and what was reasonable with the exorcism team. The religious experts were very sceptical of the benefits of exorcism in this case. In the end, after much persistence and persuasion from Professor Mannheim, the bishop sought permission for the exorcism from the highest authorities in the Anglican Church. To the surprise of both Bishop Gibot and Father Sage, permission was forthcoming from the very highest authority in the church without delay. So, with the bishop's grudging assent, Father Sage agreed that it would do no harm to try an exorcism, if only to reassure the learned professor.

This was how Father Sage found himself approaching the wide double doors of the old Irish Centre. He had agreed to meet Professor Mannheim outside of the main doors. He carried with him the various accoutrements of a routine exorcism. He had only carried out a handful of exorcisms in the previous decades. Most had achieved a modest degree of peace of mind for those troubled enough to ask for it. Father Sage considered most of these a form of blessing which helped for psychological reasons rather than expulsion of any physical and supernatural demon.

Father Sage carried with him a small leather bag. He usually kept the ceremony of exorcism as simple as possible. He only took a Bible, a small vial of holy water, and a black scarf. Professor Mannheim arrived several minutes late and opened the large, wooden double doors with an old key on a large bundle. On the stone steps stood two empty bottles of alcoholic drinks labelled WKD. *Ironic marketing labels for the occasion. Is this Satan's little joke?* thought Father Sage. The door swung slowly open without a sound. Inside was almost completely dark. Professor Mannheim had brought a small torch, which he switched on in the lobby, casting a weak light into the darkness. Professor Mannheim closed the door softly behind them.

"Follow me, Father. I'll show you to the main hall." Professor Mannheim led the way. They walked carefully, avoiding black puddles of what appeared to be standing water in the darkness. The cool, damp air on Father Sage's face was pleasant. There was a faint, sweet aroma. Like a cross between fresh paint, incense, and fuel. *All slightly incongruous and not at all reassuring in such a neglected building*, thought Father Sage.

Professor Mannheim entered a small, circular, central hall, which had several doors leading off into dark recesses. In the centre of the hall was a sturdy wooden table. It seemed to have been used relatively recently and was free from dust. In the dim lamplight, Father Sage could make out chairs set in a circle around the outside of the hall, perhaps twenty or thirty chairs in total. Behind the chairs, against one wall, many large boxes were stacked. Father Gibot noticed some form of hazard safety label on each box. Father Sage hoped that the boxes were not dangerous in any way. The boxes seemed a recent addition because they appeared quite clean and free from dust compared to the rest of the hall.

"This is the central hall, Father. I think this is the best place for the exorcism," Professor Mannheim whispered and placed his electric lamp on the table.

Father Sage placed the leather bag on the table and opened it carefully. He took out his small Bible, opened it at the marked section, and placed it on the table. Next he took out the scarf or tippet and draped it over his neck. Finally he took out the holy water.

"I will proceed, Professor. This will take up to half an hour. You may have a seat if you wish," Father Sage advised.

Professor Mannheim moved off to Father Sage's right side and sat at the edge of the room in darkness after dusting off one of the chairs with his hand.

Both Father Sage and Professor Mannheim were startled to hear movement and coughing from a corner of the room off to his left. A voice emerged from the dark corner.

"Hello, Father. How have you been?" A low, hoarse voice issued from the darkness in the corner.

Father Sage peered into the almost-black gloom of the hall but could not make out the source of the voice.

"Who is there?" Father Sage's voice trembled slightly. Professor Mannheim shone his torch towards the voice.

From the corner of the room, a small light appeared. A man was lighting a cigarette stub with a shaky hand. The torchlight revealed the outline of a figure sitting on the floor on an old sleeping bag. Father Sage could just make out that this was a dishevelled man in a long, dirty coat, seemingly rather old, with a heavy beard growth. His clothes were in shreds and heavily stained. Smoke arose from his cigarette, which glowed an orange glow as he inhaled.

"Who are you, and how did you get in here? It's not safe to live in this building," said Father Sage, forcing his voice to remain steady.

"Oh, I don't live here, Father. You woke me up. I only came in to have some rest." The man on the floor laughed a croaking, hoarse laugh and started coughing. His fit of coughing escalated until Father Sage thought he might choke and moved towards the man with an outstretched hand.

"Don't touch me. Don't come near me," croaked the man. "I don't need your help. Never have and never will." He shrank back from Father Sage's outstretched hand.

"It's all right. I won't touch you if you don't want me to," Father Sage said in an attempt to reassure the old man. "I just wanted to make sure you were okay."

"It's you who needs to worry, Father," said the old man. "You're the one who will need some help soon."

Father Sage paused to consider this warning. *Help? What sort of help?* he thought silently.

"Death is all around us. Death and destruction. I can feel it in my bones. There are bad things going on which none of us can stop," continued the old man in a deep, rough voice.

What a total nutcase, thought Father Sage.

There was a loud crack, and a bright streak of light shot from the ceiling as several roof beams and large blocks of masonry fell suddenly from the roof into the centre of the hall and onto the table below, allowing sunlight to pierce the gloom from above. Some electric wires flapped past Father Sage's face as the ceiling lights crashed onto the tiled floor. Sparks flew into the air, and small flames sprang from several of the puddles on the floor. Father Sage remembered the faint, sweet smell of fuel on entering the building. *Some of these puddles are not water*, he realised. The flames quickly rose, and within seconds the choking smoke and heat were unbearable.

Father Sage could not see the old man or Professor Mannheim, but he could hear movement getting rapidly fainter. Possibly someone running. Only one exit presented itself back the way he had come, and Father Sage took it, stumbling over the debris of a century of neglect. The main door stood ajar, and Father Sage emerged into bright sunshine. Smoke was billowing from the roof of the building and seeping from the front door and several broken windows. Neither Professor Mannheim nor the old tramp was anywhere to be seen. A call to the fire brigade was essential and urgent. Father Sage ran up the hill towards the cathedral where the refectory was open for trade.

"There is a fire in the Irish Centre! Please call the fire brigade. There might be men trapped inside the building! Call an ambulance as well. Please hurry!" shouted Father Sage to the astonished refectory staff and customers.

Several hours later, Father Sage was sitting on the cathedral steps a few metres from where the Irish Centre had been. His face and his dog collar were blackened from the smoke. All traces of the Irish Centre were gone. In their place was a rectangle of blackened and smoking uneven ground. The entire building had been consumed in fire. Several fire tenders surrounded the place where the building once stood.

A smoke-blackened fireman approached Father Sage with his helmet in his hand.

"Father, we can find no trace of anyone or any bodies in the remains of the centre. Nobody could have survived the blaze, and there would have been traces of any fatality. I can only suggest that your colleague managed to get out before you."

Father Sage ran his hand over his eyes. What a relief. At least nobody died. Although it was astounding that the old man had managed to get out.

"Thank you so much," he replied to the fireman.

It was only a few hundred metres' walk from the cathedral to the University School of Irish Studies. The day after the fire, Father Sage walked through the glass and metal front door of the school. The concrete-and-glass building was not wearing well and was looking beyond its true age. Such is the lot of academic buildings from the twentieth century in Britain. In the lobby the building manager indicated the list of academics on the wall, with attached photographs of all senior academic staff. Father Sage searched the notice board for Professor Gregory Mannheim.

"I am looking for Gregory Mannheim, professor of Irish studies. I met him yesterday at the Irish Centre before the fire," Father Sage said to the building manager.

The building manager consulted his computer screen for a few moments.

"Ah, yes. Professor Mannheim is away at present, sir," confirmed the official. "I think he has gone abroad. I am not sure when he will be back. Quite often the academic staff spend months away on research out of term time."

Father Sage was disappointed but relieved. At least Professor Mannheim was unharmed. An exorcism, a fire, a crazy tramp predicting Armageddon, and now the professor had disappeared without any communication. *It is time for some rest and a healthy dose of prayer and reflection for me,* he decided.

Dr Watson was on duty for the accident and emergency department at the Royal Victoria Infirmary. As the duty consultant, it was unusual for him to need to see patients early in their stay at the hospital. The junior- and middle-ranking medical staff were competent to manage most situations. When Dr Watson received the call to see a patient in the emergency department from his colleague Dr Cassidy, his interest was definitely aroused. Dr Cassidy and Dr Watson were standing at the workstation, scrutinising the blood tests for a patient recently admitted.

"We were definitely treating this admission as a routine case of dehydration due to gastroenteritis initially," explained Dr Cassidy. "Paramedics picked up this elderly gentleman in the city centre two days ago. A member of the public had called in because the patient seemed so ill in the street. On admission, he was severely dehydrated and suffering from severe diarrhoea and vomiting. He was barely conscious and was muttering something about a house fire. We could not get any clear medical history from him, and he had no documents from which we could identify him.

"Fluid replacement therapy did not improve his situation overnight, and we were surprised to find that his initial blood tests revealed signs of severe bone marrow syndrome. His skin has since started to deteriorate rapidly. All of his blood cell numbers are severely depleted, and with this level of white cells and haemoglobin, I am surprised he even made it to the hospital."

"Are we aware of any past treatment with chemo-therapy or radiotherapy?" asked Dr Watson.

"That is the problem," answered Dr Cassidy. "We have no past history, no name, no way of identifying him. He lost consciousness in the first twenty-four hours and has deteriorated since then. I fear we will lose him today."

"Okay. Well, I think you are doing everything you can. Continue supportive therapy with IV fluid re-placement. We can transfuse if the bloods fall any lower. Let's get him moved to the intensive care unit and ask the haematologists to see him as soon as possible," advised Dr Watson.

The strenuous medical efforts of the medi-cal team were unsuccessful. The unnamed elderly man died less than twenty-four hours later. With no means of identifying him and no relatives to contact, his death caused little interest. The medical cause of death was identified as bone marrow depression of unknown cause. Nobody considered it necessary to undertake more testing for exposure to ionising radiation or to alert the authorities about a possible radiation hazard.

Professor Gregory Mannheim was travelling in northern Norway when he became ill. He was taking a long-planned vacation in the hope of seeing the Northern Lights. Around the time that the elderly man was admitted to hospital, Professor Mannheim started to suffer from diarrhoea and vomiting. He was with a group of tourists on the border of Norway and Finland.

It was 3:00 a.m. local time, and they were five hours' drive from the nearest medical facility. The temperature was twenty-two degrees Celsius below zero. All of the tourists were clothed in full bodysuits to protect against the severe chill. These were cumbersome to put on and take off. The trip was successful in that there was a spectacular display of Northern Lights on that night. However, none of the tourists were very interested in this because Professor Mannheim was so ill that the trip had to be curtailed. His projectile vomiting was very unpleasant for the group in a small van. However, his severe diarrhoea inside his bodysuit was an even more difficult logistical challenge for them all.

The driver did his best to get Professor Mannheim to hospital in Tromso, in northern Norway, as quickly as possible. Despite his best efforts, Professor Mannheim was unconscious on arrival at the hospital. Urgent medical tests and IV therapy failed to arrest Professor Mannheim's decline, and he died two hours after arrival at the hospital. Blood tests revealed postmortem that Professor Mannheim had suffered from severe bone marrow depression with severe destruction of the lining of his gastrointestinal tract. Professor Mannheim had no significant previous medical history. His death was attributed to bone marrow depression of unknown cause.

Gerard Harrison was on his way to meet with Father Joseph Sage about the fire. The fire at the Irish Centre had caused quite a stir in the city. There was a large community of Irish descent in the city, and any possibility of political scandal would whet the appetite of the locals. *The Daily Post* would be running a series of articles on the fire and the history of Irish relations in the city.

Gerard found Father Sage in the cathedral, tidying up after a mass. They made their way to one of the small raised balconies which look onto the nave. These were usually deserted and very quiet. Good locations for an interview between a local journalist and the university chaplain.

"Many thanks for meeting me today, Father," opened Gerard. "*The Post* wants to run an article on the fire and the events leading up to it."

"Call me Joseph, please. Very happy to help out if I can, Gerard," replied Father Sage.

"So tell me how you came to be in the Irish Centre at the time of the fire, Joseph?"

"It was a rather unusual situation," started Joseph. "You see, Professor Mannheim from the university had approached me to undertake an exorcism. The professor was convinced that some sort of demons had possessed the Centre. He wanted to refurbish it and get it up and running again. He and his predecessors had tried for years to fix it up without luck. I tried to dissuade him, but he eventually convinced the bishop and those in charge, and I was asked to do the exorcism. We were in the centre just starting the ceremony when part of the roof fell in and started an electrical fire. There was some petrol or other fuel in there, and the place went up in flames in a matter of minutes. We were lucky to get out alive."

"It was just you and the professor in the building, then?" asked Gerard.

"No, actually there was also an old tramp sleeping in there. He woke just as the fire started. I am surprised he got out too, but the firefighters assured me that all three of us got out alive."

The two men talked for a further half hour about the fire and the nature of exorcism in the twenty-first century. Gerard Harrison thanked Joseph and walked back to his office in the riverside *Daily Post* building.

He tried to contact Professor Mannheim several times over the following week without success. The professor was on leave, and the university had no contact details. The task of finding the old street vagrant was difficult, if not impossible. Without a name or description, Gerard came up against a blank wall. It seemed that the fire was just one of those unexplained accidents which occur from time to time.

CHAPTER 5

CONFESSION

The sacrament of confession is one of the five sacramental rites of the Anglican Church. This is the means by which faithful Anglicans obtain forgiveness for sins committed against God and against their neighbours. By this sacrament, Christians believe they are freed from sins committed after baptism. Christian theology regarding the forgiveness of sins debates whether, at the time of judgement of the individual after their death, Christ would allow those with unconfessed mortal sins a chance to repent and save themselves. The Code of Canon Law states that a priest alone is the minister of the sacrament of confession.

Christians believe that performing confession and penance absolves them of punishment in the afterlife and reconciles them with God. Some branches of Christianity believe that everyone should confess their sins to a priest at least once a year. Other branches follow the principle that all may, some should, but none *must* confess their sins. If a Christian dies without recently or ever having been to confession, the church teaches that lifetime choices determine what happens after death.

The crypt of the cathedral was quiet. It was midafternoon. At the front of the chapel sat a woman. She appeared to be weeping. She dabbed her eyes repeatedly with a small tissue. At the back of the chapel sat a man, his features obscured in the shadow. Unless you looked straight at him, it would be easy to miss the fact that he was there at all. He appeared to be leaning forwards on a stick and looking at the floor.

Bishop Gibot walked in from the corridor, nodded to the woman sitting, unlocked the confession booth, and entered, closing the door behind him. *That lady looks somehow familiar to me*, he thought to himself, searching his memory.

A few minutes later, the small sign lit up, allowing the penitent to enter the booth. The woman wiped away her tears, put her tissue in her handbag, and entered the confession booth.

"Bless me, Father, for I have sinned. It's been seven days since my last confession," said the woman.

"Tell me how you have sinned in the eyes of God," replied the bishop.

"Your Grace, I conceived a child out of wedlock, and then I considered ending the life of my unborn child."

"Did you act on these thoughts?" asked the bishop.

"No, Your Grace. However, after my son was born, I struggled severely with thoughts of revenge. The father of my son abandoned me and refused to pay towards the support and upbringing of my son."

There was a pause as if the bishop was thinking carefully about this statement. *Now I remember who she is*, he thought to himself.

"If you did not act on these thoughts, and if you truly regret these thoughts, then God forgives you," attempted the bishop.

"I have not yet acted on my impulses, Your Grace. However, I fear that I may yet act on them. My son is now grown into an adult and has made his own way. However, I feel such anger towards the father. He should have helped us both when we needed it." The woman left this statement hanging between them and then continued. "Even now I still feel that the father owes us much to help compensate us for our struggle. The father of my child is a prominent person, and his reputation would be severely damaged if I were to reveal this to the press. I am considering asking him for financial support in order to remain silent."

The bishop took a deep breath. He could see where this conversation was heading, and it was not a comfortable place.

"Perhaps...the best thing would be for you to arrange to meet me privately at a later date, and we can discuss this in a more thoughtful way," suggested the bishop.

"Well, Your Grace, I could do this, but it would need to be quite soon. Otherwise, my temptation to reveal damaging information might overcome me," offered the woman.

"I suggest you telephone my secretary, Charles Lambert, at the bishop's lodge. Charles will arrange everything without delay," promised the bishop.

There was a rustling from the confession booth, and the woman opened the door. She glanced around the crypt and did not see anyone else waiting. She whispered quickly before closing the door. "I am hoping for a very speedy resolution to this problem, Your Grace."

As the woman walked out of the crypt, the bishop's head sank into his hands. He was sweating profusely. His mind raced as he replayed the short conversation with this woman. How had she traced him? Was she really sure? Was it really her? What was the best way forward?

In the shadowed recess at the back of the crypt, the elderly man sat still and watched.

Father Sage walked around the circular cathedral nave. Sunlight cast multicoloured patches on the walls and side chapels. He entered the confession booth. It was one week after the confession received by the Bishop.

In one of the galleries overlooking the nave, sat a man, his features obscured by the shadow covering the gallery. He appeared to be looking intently at the confession booth across the nave.

A middle aged lady entered the booth.

"Bless me, Father, for I have sinned," said the woman.

"Tell me how you have sinned in the eyes of God," replied Joseph.

"Father, I have thoughts of revenge against the father of my son, who abandoned us before he was born."

"Have you actually taken an steps in this matter?" asked Joseph.

"Yes, I have threatened the man and blackmailed him for money," said the lady.

"Did you receive any money?" asked Joseph.

"No. I have not followed through. I regret asking for the money now. The man involved is a very senior priest in the church. I don't want to damage the church. I just want to drop the whole matter."

What is this leading to, thought Joseph.

"If truly regret your thoughts, then God forgives you," said Joseph.

"I still feel very bitter towards the bish ... towards the priest involved," said the woman.

Joseph paused that thought carefully before responding.

"One way forward might be to meet this man again and ask him if he regrets his actions. If he says he does, and if you believe him, then you may be able to forgive him. Forgiving is a very healing act. This might put your mind at rest," suggested Joseph.

"Thank you, Father, I will do as you suggest," replied the lady.

Joseph could hear sounds of weeping, then the sound of the booth door opening and closing.

Sometimes I wonder if I am a social worker or a psychologist rather than a priest, thought Joseph to himself.

In the dark gallery across the nave, the elderly man sat and watched.

CHAPTER 6

GENDER

Gender theory, which separates gender from biological sex, contradicts church teaching, threatens
family, and the Christian faith.
—Dutch cardinal reporting to assembly of
Catholics in Rome, 2019

Senior tax professional fired from Centre for Global
Development for claiming that "men cannot change
into women."
—*Breitbart London,* 2019

17-year-old pupil removed from school because he
claims there are only two genders.
—*Scottish Sun,* 2019

British Labour Party suspends campaigner because
he claimed that "women don't haved——cks."
—*Breitbart London,* 2018

We hurt our boys by calling something toxic masculinity because women can be pretty f——ing toxic too.
—Oscar-winning actress, 2019

Gender is no longer a biological concept. It is a complex social system. There is a conservative backlash growing against this "progressive" idea.
—*Lancet Medical Journal*, London, England, 2019

Vatican condemns sociological "gender theory" and supports the Christian vision of a human person, created by God as male and female.
—*Vatican's congregation for Catholic Education*, 2019

Yale Law School withdraws funds from students who work for Christian nonprofit organisations.
—*Campus Reform Magazine*, 2019

Father Joseph Sage was attending a meeting with the bishop and a lay manager from the diocese office which was under the cathedral next to the university chaplaincy. The manager who had organised the meeting kicked off the proceedings with the introductions.

"Thank you for coming today, Father Sage. I am Lyndsey Joel. I am the gender violence prevention and support manager attached to the university chaplaincy and the cathedral. Just to set the context, we called this meeting after we were informed that you had discussed the use of transgender pronouns in one of your sermons last month. We have received anonymous informal complaints from parishioners. We are meeting to discuss your sermon and its effect on parishioner relations. For the record, the people present at this meeting are Bishop Leonard Gibot, Father Joseph Sage, and myself. This is an informal meeting. I will be recording the meeting, and I will produce notes for us all after the meeting." Ms Joel indicated towards a recording device on the desk in front of her.

The meeting was in one of the administration offices below the cathedral. Father Sage had received an invitation to the meeting from the bishop without any explanation and at very short notice. This was unusual since he and the bishop rarely met. They had different ideas about their religion, but there was seldom any need for them to have a conversation. Father Sage noticed that the purple colour of the bishop's clothing matched closely the vivid purple colour of Ms Joel's brutally short hair. Since he had not been informed of the subject matter in advance, he had arrived with an open mind.

"I see," replied Father Sage after a pause, and without really seeing the point at all. "I am a little taken aback. I was not aware of the reason for the meeting in advance. I have not been given an opportunity to see these alleged complaints. Would it not be best for me to see the complaints first?" he asked.

"Since this is still at the informal stage, I think we should proceed," continued Ms Joel, without explaining why she thought this would be fair or reasonable. "Now, perhaps you could start by outlining what you actually said in the sermon in question last month, Father Sage. We are referring to the sermon in which you raised to topic of gender identity and personal pronouns such as 'he' and 'she.'"

Why is this layperson being allowed to say any of this? thought Joseph. *Priests run churches, and we answer to the diocese, the bishop, and the archbishop. Laypeople should serve the clergy, not the other way around.*

The word "informal" sounded quite encouraging to Father Sage. He allowed this slightly dubious excuse to suppress his inclinations to refuse further discussion, insist on seeing any complaint before responding, and ask for a representative to be present.

"Well, from memory, the points I was making in the sermon regarding gender were that men are not women and women are not men, even though some now claim this to be the case. I pointed out that I don't think that being a woman is a matter of feeling like a woman. It is a matter of objective and simple biology. The ideology which totally detaches gender from biological sex reduces the body to a secondary status as something not essential for the human person.

"I explained that the Christian view is entirely in accord with the scientific view with the added dimension that the human person is a union of the spiritual and material world. The physical aspect of a human cannot be separated from the whole. We—that is, we Christians—believe in the principle of *corpore e anima unus*, or the union of soul and body. I quoted from Genesis 1:27. God made man in his own image. 'Man and female he created them.' I outlined that the remedy for discrimination against women, if this occurs, is not denying the biological identity of men and women but recognition that both men and women are individuals with equal dignity and value, both created in the image of God, and both deserving of equal opportunities. I was explaining that intelligent people who are objective and rational in other matters are tying themselves in knots to avoid the truth that men cannot simply change into women because it might hurt the feelings of a tiny minority of people who don't want this to be true.

"I spoke for a short time about the recent example of a man who defines himself as a trans woman who was jailed for violent crimes and was moved to a male prison after he sexually assaulted women in a female prison. I alluded to the fact that more women could be harmed if we accept this fantastic nonsense to be promulgated as truth."

"Yes. I believe that you stated that a man's internal feelings that he is a woman have no basis in material reality. Can you see that might have been seen as problematic by some parishioners? Maybe even threatening to them?" asked Ms Joel.

Father Sage was not easily able to make this rather large leap of logic. He paused to consider his reply. "I don't see how someone would rationally think it was threatening. I could see how it might challenge their existing beliefs and preferences, but for me that's an important and positive part of our role. To challenge our parishioners when we encounter ideas that contradict our fundamental values is a positive feature. I don't know who this complaint came from, and I would be interested to see the original complaint, or complaints, because I don't have any context as to what exactly their objection was," replied Father Sage.

"Sorry to interrupt," Bishop Gibot said, "but can I just ask Father Sage to provide us with a copy of the full sermon? I'd like to read the whole thing. If you could just give us the whole document, this would be helpful to me."

"Yes, of course, Your Grace," replied Father Sage. "I will certainly send you a copy of my sermon. It might also help if you access a YouTube debate which first alerted me to this problem. The YouTube debate is between two professors in North America. They debate the use of personal pronouns and using gendered language."

"Could you provide a link for the YouTube video?" asked Ms Joel.

"Certainly, I can provide this link for you. I will send it over with the text of my sermon. It was from a programme debating gender concepts. I referred to this debate in my sermon. My parishioners seemed very interested. After the service, several parishioners stayed behind, and we debated this in some depth. There were a range of opinions, but this was a very friendly debate. It was my understanding that several of them wanted to research this matter further. Obviously, the people who had an issue did not express any discontent to me at the time. I am puzzled why nobody spoke to me about concerns," continued Father Sage.

"Just to give you some context about the debate in question," said Ms Joel, more to the bishop than to Father Sage, "the professor Father Sage refers to is a rather extreme alt-right figure. He is involved in an extreme alt-right website which has been involved in raising hundreds of thousands of dollars for his research. Some time ago, he gave a lecture in which he identified student protesters by posting their social media accounts so people would bully and threaten them online. He lectures criticising feminism, critiquing trans-rights, and supporting white supremacy."

"I see that you already know of this academic. I am not sure you are entirely right about his public speaking or his political status," replied Father Sage. "But the thing is, we cannot shield our parishioners from these ideas. Am I supposed to comfort them and make sure that they are insulated from ideas like this? Is that what the point of this meeting is? Because to me that is contrary to our role as moral and pastoral leaders. I was not taking sides personally in this debate. I was presenting both arguments and trying to give our parishioners a balanced view of the Christian perspective as well as the scientific view."

"If you are presenting something like this, you have to think about the kind of climate that you're creating. These arguments are counter to our human rights code. It is discriminatory to be targeting someone due to their gender identity or gender expression. So bringing something like that up in a sermon—and to do so in a manner that does not employ critical thinking—is a mistake," Ms Joel responded. She seemed to have reached a fairly clear conclusion already.

Surely a layperson should not be lecturing the bishop and me about my sermons, thought Joseph. *I don't have to explain myself to this idiot. The bishop should have stepped in and fired her already.*

"I was critical and balanced in my presentation. I introduced the subject critically in my sermon. Both sides of the argument were explored fully. I did not threaten anyone's human rights. Most especially the right of everyone to free speech was particularly preserved," asserted Father Sage.

"Presenting both sides of the argument is all very well. However, misgendering is a problematic idea that we should unpack," suggested Ms Joel.

"By 'unpack,' I assume you mean 'prevent'? But if I had just stated that misgendering was the problem, I would have been taking one side only and presenting a conclusion without the debate, and not presenting a balanced idea or the Christian perspective," suggested Father Sage.

"Yes." Ms Joel's single-word response left little to the imagination and explained very little. It seemed that she expected Father Sage to take a side, as long as it was her side of the argument.

"But simply stating that misgendering was wrong would be taking sides as far as I am concerned. If I had said that everything that came out of the on-line debate was nonsense but I suggest you watch the YouTube lecture anyway, it would have been ridiculous," said Father Sage.

"Okay. So I understand your positionality. But the reality is that you have created a toxic climate for some of our parishioners," said Ms Joel.

"Positionality. What does that even mean? Is it even a real word? Toxic climate? For whom? How many complained? Who complained? One? Ten? A hundred?" asked Father Sage, looking rather bewildered and becoming slightly more resistant.

"Please don't interrupt me, Father Sage. Let me speak," countered Ms Joel, implying that she had been prevented from speaking. As far as Father Sage could discern, nothing had prevented her from speaking.

"I have no idea how many people complained or what their complaint was. You haven't shown me the complaints. Surely I have a right to see the complaints," said Father Sage, aiming this at the bishop.

"Yes, I understand that this is upsetting for you, but there are issues of confidentiality," responded Ms Joel before the bishop could comment.

"Are you saying that the number of people complaining is confidential?" asked Father Sage, incredulous.

"Yes," Ms Joel confirmed without seeming to feel the need to justify this dubious assertion. It seemed that something was confidential if Ms Joel decided it was so.

"Okay," replied Father Sage while really thinking, *What a load of nonsense.*

"One or multiple parishioners have come forwards saying that this is something that they were concerned about and that it made them uncomfortable," Ms Joel said. "If this person were, for example, a trans person who complained, you were basically debating whether or not that trans person should have rights within our society. That's not something that is really acceptable in the context of the kind of environment that we're trying to create in our church or university. It was the equivalent of debating whether or not a parishioner of colour should have rights or should be allowed to be married. Do you see how this is not something about which we are intellectually neutral or about which we are willing to debate? I mean, this is about fundamental rights and freedoms. Such debates should not be permitted at all."

"I was not debating race at all. Surely, denial of biological reality should be up for debate. Many people around the world are debating it. We are debating it now. If we don't debate and just pretend that we agree with the view that gender no longer exists in physical reality, then we are being dishonest. We surely have a right to freedom of expression and an obligation to be honest about real issues," said Father Sage.

"You are welcome to your own opinions, Father Sage. But when you're bringing it into the context of the sermon, that can become problematic for us, and that creates an unsafe environment for parishioners," Ms Joel continued.

"Out in the real world, our parishioners are exposed to these ideas every day. I don't see how I'm doing a disservice to my parishioners by exposing them to ideas that are already out in the public domain. This interview process is really very stressful for me. It does not feel at all informal, and your suggestions seem contrary to Christian values," Father Sage said.

"Can we mention the Gender and Sexual Violence Policy?" asked Ms Joel, aiming this question to Bishop Gibot and ignoring Father Sage's question.

"Yes, indeed, please do," suggested the bishop enthusiastically. He was glad to have something simple to contribute.

"Under that policy, gender violence doesn't just include sexual violence, but it also includes the targeting of people based on gender. So this includes transphobia, biphobia, and homophobia. All those sorts of things are defined as gender violence and are protected from criticism and violence under our policy. We are responsible for not impacting our parishioners in that way and not spreading transphobia amongst our worshippers," suggested Ms Joel.

"I have a real problem with this line of questioning. I didn't target anybody. I did not spread any form of phobia. Nobody objected to me that they felt targeted. Who do you think I targeted?" asked Father Sage.

"Trans people," confirmed Ms Joel. She seemed to think that this fact was indisputable.

"How? By telling them about ideas that are already circulating widely in society? By telling them that there are two sides to this debate? By quoting fundamental Christian values from our most sacred scripture?" Father Sage felt this conversation was becoming surreal.

"It's not just about telling them things. By discussing something in a balanced manner and legitimizing something as a valid perspective, even if you balance this with a different idea as an equally valid perspective, some people will feel threatened," suggested Ms Joel.

"Surely part of my role is to present all perspectives—" asked Father Sage.

"That's not necessarily accurate, Father Sage, when you are triggering people or making people feel threatened as a result," stated Ms Joel.

"Well, this is something that's being debated in current society, and I don't feel the need to shield people from what's going on in society," Father Sage said.

"Okay, so to give you some context, also circulating at present in society we see literature which debates whether we should have white supremacy currently. There is another debate in society about white supremacy and ethnic cleansing. Would you raise this issue in a sermon and present white supremacy and nonwhite supremacy as valid perspectives?" asked Ms Joel.

"If it was relevant to the context of the overall sermon, then maybe I would raise the topic of racial integration," suggested Father Sage. "It depends on the context. I would never endorse white supremacy or black supremacy, but I might raise the subject in order to promote Christian values of equal opportunity. However, I was not talking about racial supremacy views in my sermon. If there are really ideas that are being debated in society, we should be presenting these to our parishioners in the context of our Christian values. I don't see what's transphobic about discussing the real issue of transgender people. It's a real issue with real consequences," countered Father Sage.

"It is a real issue. But it is a real issue that targets trans people by threatening them and giving out their personal information so that they can be attacked and harassed and so that death threats will be made against them. I don't want to suggest we compare everything to Hitler, but what you did is like neutrally showing a speech by Hitler and pretending that his views were balanced views. This is the kind of thing that is diametrically opposed to everything that we endorse. Could I ask why you really wanted to raise this topic? Was this just a provocative act of rebellion against our gender policy?" asked Ms Joel.

"No, of course not. I was talking about gendered language, the Christian attitude towards gender, and the societal context of this whole issue," confirmed

Father Sage. "So I really cannot understand how this can be seen as transphobic. Also it has nothing whatever to do with Hitler and the Nazis. By virtue of me just exposing people to an idea, I don't understand why you have attached that label to me. I really don't."

"It's more about the effect than the intention. Obviously, I accept that wasn't your intention if you say so," said Ms Joel unconvincingly. "But nevertheless it disturbed and upset parishioners enough for them to complain."

"So everything stems from a single anonymous parishioner who feels threatened? Everything has to be changed to cater to this single anonymous person? Is this right?" asked Father Sage.

"Can I offer a different perspective?" suggested the bishop, ignoring and deflecting Father Sage's question. "Was your sermon really looking at grammar? Was it focused on the use of personal pronouns such as 'he' and 'she'? And am I not correct in saying that grammar is not really something that's a suitable subject of discussion or debate in a religious sermon? Should we not leave grammar to English teachers?"

"But this issue is the subject of a huge debate in society right now," replied Father Sage. "The use of words, the meaning of those words, and the ideas those words express in the context of words written in our sacred scripture—these are all very relevant to my role. The traditional Christian view of gender is very relevant to this debate. There is no mention of 'ze' in the bible, just 'he' and 'she.' Jesus changed water into wine but not men into women."

"Did you know that there are some countries where you could be imprisoned if you misgendered someone?" suggested the bishop ominously. "Let me take another tack and use an example. Some climate change deniers suggest that that all views have an equal value. Of course, scientists never proclaim one hundred percent validity for any idea because the scientific method cannot demonstrate anything with absolute certainty. That's the nature of scientific inquiry, including the social sciences. Some people believe that fossil fuels do not contribute to global warming, but that is not a credible, academic, scholarly, scientific position. So to present something as if there are two equally valid sides to a debate when this is not credible is problematic. I'm approaching this from the point of view of the church. We must not legitimise positions that don't have credible evidence. Just like claims of white racial supremacy are not credible and we should avoid mentioning them. There is also the issue that certain groups of parishioners will be subject to what the majority thinks which will make them feel threatened."

This rather chaotic set of examples did not seem to clarify anything in Father Sage's mind.

"But this gender issue is already in the public domain, and both points of view do have significant validity, and both are relevant to Christian teaching of gender and marriage," suggested Father Sage.

"Yes, this is in the public domain, and there are a lot of people of an alt-right perspective who give these views too much legitimacy," suggested the bishop. "The Nazis actually used the issue of free speech in 1920s Weimar Germany as an argument for their ideas. By discussing some ideas, we give them greater credibility. Therefore such discussion should be prevented. There are limits to free speech, after all. This is more important than free speech. There are public figures like Hitler who bring hatred, who target groups, and who should be avoided. If you look statistically, the level of suicide attempts that trans people suffer is the highest of any group in society. Ideas are in the public domain, and people are going to engage with these ideas, but we have to also think of the atmosphere we create for our parishioners.

"The concept of the tyranny of the majority is relevant to this context and is one which we need to avoid. We want to create an environment which is comfortable for everyone, which does not cause offense or threaten anyone, and which does not block people out just because they are the minority in a particular group. Otherwise they might not feel comfortable voicing their opinion. You are a representative of the church when you deliver your sermon. Do you understand how this could become an issue? I understand why you chose your subject. You wanted to present this as an issue, to talk about it, and to bring out the Christian perspective. But you must try to understand what the impact of that choice was and why that might have not been the best choice for this context. Another subject—a safer subject—might have been wiser."

"I suppose I can see why people might think that the subject matter was unconventional. I probably wouldn't present this again in exactly the same way." Father Sage offered this as an olive branch but without much enthusiasm. The fact that it was two against one was beginning to erode his confidence.

"But you would do something similar again, wouldn't you? It's your principle to present a completely balanced view of everything, isn't it?" asked the bishop.

"Not quite. Not every view has equal validity, obviously. However, I am happy to offer my parishioners a view with which I disagree and explain that I am open to listening to people with different points of view while confirming the Christian perspective, of course. I think you will find that most Christian priests do have a firm belief in the Christian point of view," replied Father Sage, glancing at Ms Joel.

"So your position is that the people who complained were wrong?" asked the bishop.

"I'm not saying they were wrong. I have not seen what they actually say in their complaint, after all. You haven't shown the complaint to me, so how can I say they were wrong if I cannot see what they say? I'm suggesting they may not be open to a new perspective and I might help them to understand another perspective. If you just show me the complaint, I can reach a view," replied Father Sage.

"Do you understand how what happened was contrary to…sorry, Lyndsey, what was the policy called again?" asked the bishop, scratching his head.

"The Gender and Sexual Violence Policy," replied Ms Joel, brandishing a bundle of paper proudly.

"The Gender and Sexual Violence Policy. Yes, quite. Do you understand how—"

"Sorry, I really don't see what I violated. What did I violate in that policy exactly?" asked Father Sage, interrupting the bishop.

"You committed gender-based violence, exhibited transphobia, and caused harm to trans people by suggesting that their identity as invalid or their pronouns are invalid—or potentially invalid—and you threatened their existence in doing so," said Ms Joel, reading extracts from the policy triumphantly.

"So you're saying I caused harm and violence by raising an issue which is relevant to church teaching and is widely being debated in the public sphere? It seems to me that the policy you have is contrary to fundamental Christian values, not to mention common sense and free speech," suggested Father Sage.

"This is a protected issue which society, the church, and the university hold as a value," replied Ms Joel.

"Well, if by raising a commonly discussed matter, quoting Christian beliefs, and referring people to online information, I am transphobic and causing harm and violence, then so be it. I can do nothing to control that. The problem lies with the policy and not with me," said Father Sage, leaning back in his chair and looking towards the ceiling.

"So that's not something you have an issue with? The fact that this happened? Are you sorry that it happened?" asked Ms Joel.

"I know in my heart that I'm not transphobic, and I know I didn't express any kind of political view or cause any form of violence. I presented this entire debate in a very neutral manner. I feel this entire discussion we are having is based on a falsehood. Should I say that I am sorry when I don't think I have done anything wrong?" replied Father Sage.

"That's really the problem. To present information like this neutrally can help cultivate an environment where these kinds of opinions—alt-right opinions, white supremacist opinions, antitrans opinions, antigay opinions, antiwomen opinions, misogynist opinions—are encouraged. It creates a culture where those kinds of opinions can be nurtured and created. There are some subjects we should raise in church and some we should not. There are environments when it might be safe to discuss white supremacist issues because the audience have more critical faculties. For something of this nature, it is not appropriate to raise it in a general sermon to a group of all ages and all abilities," suggested Ms Joel.

"I understand what you mean about framing, context, and making our presentations appropriate relevant to the audience," offered Father Sage. At last they had found a simple concept about which they could agree.

"Well, that's good that you acknowledge that, especially since you're saying that misgendering is not something that you agree with and not something that you're trying to promote. You say it's just that you're trying to open up a debate. But the problem is that the specific debate is about whether trans people are not even people. That is not a debate which would be compatible with our policy. Does that make sense?" asked Ms Joel.

Father Sage considered expressing his true sentiments—that this whole issue was a pile of garbage. *Perhaps not*, he thought.

"I don't really think the topic is about whether trans people are people. The issue is about use of language, the reality of objective biological facts, and fundamental Christian values. You cannot extend it to an issue of personhood. I did present the point of view that some people have that by denying people their pronouns, you are denying their dignity. I stated that argument without making a judgement either way personally. And I also stated the Christian perspective that God created a man and a woman and that marriage is between a man and a woman reinforces biological reality. Since I am a Christian priest and we all work for the same Christian faith, I am sure you would expect me to at least refer in passing to the Christian doctrines?" asked Father Sage.

The interviewers seemed to be less convinced about this point of doctrine and faith.

"This is not a matter of religious belief, Father Sage. Do you understand that if you were a trans person in your congregation that day, you would have felt threatened? Or if the topic was 'Should women have the vote?' and you were a woman, do you think that might be problematic? If you were a trans person, do you not think that raising the subject might make you feel that your identity or existence as a person was being questioned and up for debate?" asked Ms Joel.

"Would I feel that way if I were a trans person? It's hard for me to say because it ties into who people are as individuals and how strong they are and how willing they are to engage with new ideas. I don't think I can make a generalization about that. If someone was attacking white men in front of me, which does happen to me quite often these days as a matter of fact, I feel strong enough in my position to either respond if I wanted to or not respond if I chose not to. I am confident enough to know inside that it is wrong to condemn all men and all white men as a group, and I am content being a white male and an individual. I might feel threatened or even offended, but I accept that others have the right of free expression of their views, even if this offends me. But I cannot say how other people might react. Indeed, everyone is likely to react individually. As a general rule, I cannot know what another person thinks or feels without asking them," replied Father Sage.

"Are you aware of confirmation bias? Have you heard that phrase?" asked Ms Joel, wagging her finger at Father Sage. She seemed to feel this was a major point in her favour.

"Yes," replied Father Sage.

"Because many of our parishioners already hold very strong opinions, whether or not these are opinions backed up with evidence," replied Ms Joel. "My point is that we have parishioners with very strong opinions about this and that, and that's fine, but if they're going to be challenged about those opinions, then that is a problem, and we should avoid doing so. We should not challenge our parishioners if this makes them feel threatened. If we claim to be an institution that prides itself on having socially relevant, evidence-based, fair, objective policies, we should avoid the kind of bias involved in promoting anything which cannot be substantiated in a credible way. We are not doing our job if we simply present both sides of every argument in a neutral way.

"The analogy of climate change is relevant again here. The fossil fuel industry knew in the 1970s about climate change. The tobacco companies knew all about lung cancer as early as the 1920s. The degree of advertising and power that the petroleum producers, big tobacco lobbies, big pharma, etcetera have through advertising and through the media just reinforces the kind of prejudices that we are discussing. Everyone is entitled to their opinions, but we have a duty as public intellectuals to make sure that we're not furthering false opinions. This whole idea about free speech and public debate about things which are not substantiated by the facts lacks credibility. I include this issue about personal pronouns.

"I don't find anything credible in those that oppose the trans pronouns. This brings me back to the next point, which is thinking about how to move forward. I can see why you made your choice of subject matter, but your role as parish priest is not really to teach parishioners about the politics of grammar. To be discussing irrelevant side issues doesn't make sense to me. Is this your general style, to discuss such side issues, or was this a departure from your normal style of sermon?" Ms Joel paused for breath.

"This was the first time I chose to discuss the subject of personal pronouns and male female identity. I just wanted to promote understanding of the topic and stimulate discussion. People expressed many opinions after my sermon," responded Father Sage.

"Okay, so would you be comfortable to stick to a more traditional subject for future sermons?" asked Ms Joel.

"Well, I would be reluctant to suppress my personality or to ignore important issues of the day. What exactly do you mean by 'more traditional' sermons? I have spoken in the past about astronomy, astrology, and many other topical subjects which have a bearing on theological Christian teaching. Could I ask whether you are even a Christian, Ms Joel?" Father Sage said.

Ms Joel seemed completely unaware of this question. At any rate she ignored it entirely.

"So let's move forward, as there seems to have been a little bit of a breakdown in communication. Do you write out your sermons, or do you just work from memory?" asked Ms Joel.

"I write them out and read from my written notes," confirmed Father Sage.

"Okay. Could you send me your written notes before you deliver your sermons, so I can have a quick look over them?" asked Ms Joel.

"I usually hand write them on paper with a pen, but I can take a picture and email this to you," responded Father Sage. "But sometimes I don't decide until just a few hours before a service. It would not really be practical to send it to you literally two minutes before I start. Also, I am not sure if it would be appropriate for you to approve my sermons or otherwise. Are you a Christian? What authority do you have over a parish priest?" replied Father Sage, turning again to look for support from the bishop.

"Okay. All right. But going forward, if you can try to plan a little further ahead, this will help. Prepare a few days ahead, and send notes to me in advance, so I can take a look at them. I will talk everything over with the bishop and other colleagues. Then we'll talk about how to move forwards with this. How does this sound?" asked Ms Joel.

"I'm sorry, but this is a little vague. Could you clarify what you mean by moving forward? That's rather general. Are you suggesting that you need to approve every sermon or homily I deliver? Are you only asking to see one sermon or them all? Is it even really appropriate for a person unqualified in theology to be determining the content of a religious sermon?" asked Father Sage, turning again to look at the bishop, who seemed increasingly uninterested in the proceedings. He seemed to prefer that Ms Joel handled the matter.

"Well, we're going to have to talk about what we have discussed and decide if you can continue. Hopefully everything can continue, and we can continue to have a working relationship. This is something that I will have to talk over with the bishop and my colleagues because frankly some of the things that we have talked about are a little bit problematic, and we need to process them before deciding," replied Ms Joel without any reference to the bishop.

She seemed to be bringing the meeting to a rather ambiguous and threatening close.

Bishop Gibot sat motionless throughout this part of the discussion and did not offer a view on the questions raised by Father Sage.

"Do you know when you might have an answer for me on these questions?" asked Father Sage.

"I do not," replied Ms Joel with an air of finality.

"So basically, you're telling me that either I accept supervision and censorship of my sermons by a lay administrator and have all sermons approved in advance by the same noncleric, or the alternative is that my job would somehow be terminated? Is this what you are threatening? I'm not sure that these grounds for termination would even be legal," suggested Father Sage.

"That is not something that is in my control. I am not your employer. I'm the person responsible for church and university policy in this area. I have to transmit my information to colleagues and discuss the matter with the bishop. If I knew what the outcome would be, then I would tell you now," confirmed Ms Joel.

"What is the process? What committee is this going to? Who is deciding the outcome? I need to know where information about me is circulating, and I don't know. I have not even seen the alleged complaint about my sermon. This is all very like a Kafka novel to me," said Father Sage.

"Right now I would say that this is an informal process, Father Sage," the bishop said. "If it became a formal process, which would be the case if somebody made a formal complaint and wanted to go forwards with it, then that would be a little different and much more serious. You would then have a right to see the complaint, of course. The formal process would be based on either the Gender Violence Policy or the Harassment and Discrimination Policy and would go through those policies and procedures, which are available to you. Hopefully, this can be resolved informally."

"That's my hope too," suggested Ms Joel. "So I guess that's what we mean by 'moving forward.' The phrase 'moving forward' means that this is an informal process. Part of the reason I wanted to hear your story is because a complaint or complaints were made, and since there are two sides, we need to hear your version."

"So there are two sides and you want to gain a balanced perspective. Just like I presented a balanced perspective in my sermon. But you don't want me to present balanced arguments when it concerns your favourite protected topics like gender. You want me to avoid speaking about these topics altogether. Also, you are unwilling to reveal the actual complaint or even confirm how many people complained. All of this seems rather unfair and arbitrary to me," suggested Father Sage.

"So if you can send me your written sermon notes, and I might need to sit in on some of your sermons, after talking it over with the bishop, just to assess and see how things are, moving forward. Do you have any other questions?" asked Ms Joel, ignoring Father Sage's objections once again.

"No, not really," replied Father Sage. "Apart from the several questions I already asked which you have ignored and which therefore remain entirely unanswered." While this was factually accurate, Father Sage found it difficult to resist a touch of sarcasm.

"OK, thanks for coming in, Father Sage. I will be in touch," finished Ms Joel, gathering her papers together on the table with an air of finality and determination.

Father Sage left the meeting with his mind in a spin. Nothing about the meeting was reassuring. It seemed that his job was on the line because he had dared to exercise his right to free speech, explain Christian principles, and challenge the gender pronoun police who were now embedded in the church. The bishop seemed unconcerned. Ms Joel seemed to have untrammelled power in this context. Father

Sage wondered where exactly this matter would end up.

After he left the room, Ms Joel turned to Bishop Gibot.

"We were right to have this meeting, Bishop. Father Sage is clearly a problem. I felt a distinct hostility from him today. He is clearly unwilling to accept church and university policy in this area. I suspect he will resist any supervision for his sermons. Father Sage seems to have a marked resistance to our diversity and equality project. I think we need to act decisively and stamp this out," suggested Ms Joel.

"Of course, Ms Joel, I will guided by you in this matter of legal policy," replied the bishop.

CHAPTER 7

THE HIRING

Hijab infant sexualisation scandal: A spokesman from Church House, the headquarters of the Church of England, did not share concerns of school inspectors in England about infant girls wearing the hijab in school.
—*Breitbart.com*, November 2017

Jail chaplain "ousted" as radical Christian: Muslim senior chaplain dismisses Christian junior chaplain from Brixton prison for "extreme" Christianity.
—*The Times*, February 2018

꜔ ꜔

B ishop Gibot shook hands with Adila Barzin.
   "Thank you for coming to meet me today, Ms Barzin," opened the bishop. "Please come and have a seat."

The bishop ushered Ms Barzin towards a comfortable chair in his office in the administration area below the cathedral.

Adila Barzin was wearing a full burqa and niqab, a garment that covered her body, head, and face. Only her eyes were visible via a slot in her veil. She had been invited to meet the bishop with regard to a possible working position within the church. She had been recommended by a contact of the bishop's who had worked in the police radicalization prevention team.

"Ms Barzin, I have invited you here today to discuss an opportunity which has arisen within the church," the bishop explained. "We are looking for someone to help us to foster and maintain good relations between the religious communities in our city. We seek someone who can speak both English and classic Arabic. You come very highly recommended, and I wanted to explore this post with you today."

"Thank you for offering me this opportunity, Your Grace. I am very grateful," replied Ms Barzin.

"I understand that you have some experience of Islam, Christianity, and Judaism in the Middle East," said the bishop.

"Yes, indeed, sir," replied Ms Barzin. "I came to England from Afghanistan with my husband a couple of years ago. We fled the conflict there. Before the fighting, the community relations were very good in Kabul. I had many friends from many different religious and cultural backgrounds."

"Excellent. Excellent, Ms Barzin. The position is a new one and will be based in the administration offices below the cathedral. If you are successful, you will have an office there, and parking is available in the underground car park. You will also have some administration support to help you to organise yourself appropriately. One thing we would like to ask of you—if you accept the post, of course—is to attend some of our services," suggested the bishop. "In an observational capacity only, of course," he added tentatively. "This will help to raise the profile of your post."

Ms Barzin had been warned about this by her sponsor, who had advised the bishop on her suitability. She was prepared.

"Yes, certainly, Your Grace," she replied. "I would be happy to observe your ceremonies. Would I be permitted to wear my religious clothing to any such ceremonies?"

"Why, yes, certainly. Of course. We will be wearing traditional Christian religious dress, as well you know. Christian priests generally like to wear Christian clothing." The bishop thought this was quite a good little joke.

Ms Barzin did not laugh.

"I would like to request a large storage room and a second administration office if this is possible," asked Ms Barzin. "I am happy to offer to bring several additional administration assistants at my own expense. They also all have full awareness of Christianity, Islam, and Judaism. My immigration sponsors are very generous people. This will save your church a significant amount on administration costs."

"Well now, that is very generous," replied the bishop. "Yes, I am sure we can find you a storage room and an administration office from which your colleagues can work. Thank you for this kind offer, Ms Barzin."

"You are so kind, Your Grace," replied Ms Barzin, bowing her head. Her broad smile was hidden beneath her veil.

"Right. Well, that is settled, then," continued the bishop. "Here is a small pack of papers for you to read. They describe the terms and conditions, salary, etcetera. If you could consider the matter carefully and let me know if you accept the post within the next week or two, I would be so grateful."

The bishop watched as Ms Barzin receded down the corridor from his office. *This is real progress*, he thought. *The minority community within the city will absolutely love me for this.*

Two days later, Ms Barzin confirmed that she would be delighted to accept the offer and she was available to start the following month.

CHAPTER 8

THE FIRING

British nurse fired for giving a Bible to a patient and asking him to sing a hymn.
  —*BBC News,* 2019

Doctor threatened with dismissal for asking Muslim woman to remove her veil.
  —*Metro Newspaper,* England, 2019

English police force refuses to employ a man because he is white, heterosexual, and male.
  —*BBC News,* 2019

Cambridge professor wins substantial damages after college fails to protect its employees from repeated hostility and violence based on race.
  —*The News Tribune,* 2019

Many decades after their ordination and several weeks before his death, Bishop Gibot invited Father Joseph Sage to the bishop's lodge to discuss his varied and widespread employment opportunities.

The large Edwardian building given to the bishop to use as his living quarters provided all domestic and social needs for bishops. It was set in the leafy suburbs of the city and looked over manicured gardens and a neat gravel driveway. It had sufficient bedrooms for a family of ten. It was originally built by a wealthy British merchant to house his granddaughter and her large family in the nineteenth century. Bishop Gibot, who was unmarried and had no children, found the building entirely suitable as a peaceful home, well away from the politics and intrigue of his professional role.

Father Sage had arrived early and was admiring the oak panelling in the entrance hall when the bishop appeared to greet him.

"Please come through to my study, Joseph." The bishop ushered Father Sage into a large room facing out onto the gardens. Both priests sat in comfortable leather armchairs facing a large bow window. "Can I offer you a sherry or a cup of tea, perhaps?"

"No, thank you, Your Grace," replied Father Joseph. "It is a little early for sherry for me, and I am trying to avoid caffeine at present. Beautiful garden. The diocese is looking after you well, Your Grace."

"Yes, indeed. We are blessed with excellent gardening staff. The rhododendrons are particularly splendid this year. I understand that the rain is the key," the bishop said as he pointed out the splendid bank of rhododendron bushes. "It has been so many years since we trained together in Selchester, Father Leonard. I recall those days of youth and freedom with great pleasure. We had an enjoyable time together, didn't we? So much has changed since then—mostly for the better, I believe."

There was a pause as the two men contemplated their different views on the changes to society and to the church over previous decades. *What alternative universe is the bishop remembering?* wondered Father Sage. *Certainly not the one that I lived in.*

"I believe that your father was a bit of a war hero," said the bishop.

"Well, yes. He did have a distinguished war record, Your Grace," replied Father Sage. *What is this leading to?* he wondered. *Bishop Gibot has never been interested in small talk with me before.*

"Yes, I did not know my father," said the bishop, staring out of the window into the garden. "He died when I was rather young. A liver complaint apparently according to my mother. She was deeply affected by the loss. She never recovered, if the truth be told. I was packed off to boarding school. Not a very pleasant experience for me. Plenty of bullying and sadistic schoolmasters. One had to learn to be very adaptable very quickly..."

There was another pause in the conversation.

"I was wondering what Your Grace wanted to discuss," Father Sage asked after the silence between them started to become uncomfortable.

"Ah, yes. Well now, then," began the bishop. "I wanted to invite you today to consider your current post in the broader context of the needs of the diocese. I have tried to consider the needs of all stakeholders. These are difficult times, and we have often to consider widely before taking any action of course. I want to start by emphasising how much I appreciate your dedicated and valuable service to the church. I am one of your greatest admirers, as you know. I have tried hard to convince my colleagues that your dedication and enthusiasm is indispensable to our cause."

There was another pregnant pause during which Father Sage wondered whether he was about to be promoted to high office.

"However, after much thought and consideration, a decision was inevitable eventually..." The bishop paused again, reluctant to finish his sentence and actually deliver the final blow.

"Indeed, Your Grace. What decision has been taken exactly?" responded Father Sage to fill the silence, still having no clear idea what the bishop was about to announce.

"Mmm. Well, you see, there are considerable financial constraints at present," intoned the bishop, staring at his feet. "As a result, some rationalisation has been necessary at all levels. In the end, this was a difficult balancing position. However, the chaplaincy priest post which you occupy at the university has always been a fixed-term post. It has therefore been necessary to bring the post to a conclusion. We… that is, I…am very grateful for your sterling efforts as well as your energy and enthusiasm. The post will in the future be shared between denominations on an ecumenical basis. I hope you will understand the pressures that have led to this decision."

There was yet another pause, during which the bishop carefully avoided eye contact with Father Sage and fixed his attention on the rhododendrons through the large picture windows again.

"So…my post is to be axed. I am losing my job. I will be unemployed. Is that right?" Father Sage broke the silence with three statements, all of which amounted to the same thing.

"I knew you would understand. There are so many conflicting demands, you see," replied the bishop hopefully.

Father Sage felt numb. He sat for what seemed like many minutes without speaking.

"This has come as a great shock to me, Your Grace. I had no warning that anything of this sort was being considered. I am very disappointed after putting so much time and effort into the chaplaincy over the past five years. Is this linked to the transgender issue about which we met recently?" Father Sage stared intently at the bishop, looking for some signs of encouragement.

Of course, it is linked to the gender nonsense, you naive buffoon, thought the bishop to himself. *The gender meeting was arranged specifically to allow me to take this action, of course.*

"Yes, I have every sympathy, Father Sage. I am sure that we will find something suitable for you very soon. No, the gender matter is completely unrelated to this decision, of course." The bishop tried to be reassuring.

The truth was otherwise, but he would never admit as much. It was very unlikely that there would be anything for Father Sage in the near future—or in the distant future, for that matter. In fact, he was determined to ensure that Father Sage was

permanently excluded from any further professional involvement with the church.

Both men sat in silence for what seemed like
many minutes. The bishop examined Father Sage,
who sat looking out of the window over a warm and
sunny, well-manicured garden with a frown on his
forehead.

"What will I do without work and an income? My
post is tied to the stipend, Your Grace. If I lose my
post, I lose my income too. I had not considered the
possibility of redundancy within the church. Have
you received adverse reports of my service to my parishioners? If so, it would only be fair to give me full
details and a chance to put matters right," pressed
Father Sage.

"No, no, no, Father," answered the bishop with
just the trace of a smile on his lips. "On the contrary.
Your service has been excellent. Absolutely excellent. Attendance in the chapel is rising, albeit from a
very low base, of course. Your predecessor really did
struggle there. I have received many positive comments from your parishioners and colleagues. I assure you, this is not personal. Not a bit of it. I realise
that we have had our doctrinal differences since our
training days. However, this plays no part in the current decision, of course. No, this is just a matter of
simple finance, Father. The diocese cannot live by

bread alone, as someone we both know well once said."

The bishop paused for Father Sage to recognise and enjoy this little joke. No response from Father Sage was forthcoming. Bishop Gibot ploughed on regardless.

"Money is our enemy in these strained times. I will be giving you at least a month to find an alternative position. Possibly a little more even if you need it. And of course, I will give you a glowing reference for your next bishop. Now, you must not worry about the future. In no time at all, you will be fixed up with something you can really get your teeth into."

Father Sage sat in silence for a few seconds, a puzzled frown on his brow. At length, he replied slowly, "I hope you are right, Bishop. I hope there is some form of employment available soon. Without this I will be homeless and unable to support myself. I wonder if I should be considering leaving the ministry altogether. Is it worth me exploring other avenues of training or employment? My apologies, Bishop, for these rather chaotic thoughts, but this is such a surprise to me."

"Yes, indeed. Absolutely right. An excellent idea," purred the bishop. "I think you are being very practical and sensible to consider all of your options. However, as I said, I am sure that there will be a post suitable for you within the church within a short time. Something you can really get your teeth into and like."

Such ambiguity is surely justified, thought the bishop. *Indeed, it is not really a lie at all*, he mused silently. It is, after all, possible that Father Sage could find an alternative post, despite his best efforts to blackball the reactionary fool. *I am not misleading Father Sage. Just bringing him down to earth gently. A very Christian act.* The bishop nodded silently as these thoughts reassured him about his dishonesty.

"Well, I do appreciate you seeing me personally to inform me of this, Your Grace," said Father Sage. "And thank you also for committing to such a positive reference to support me."

It is high time to end this meaningless conversation and speculation, thought the bishop. Father Sage had always appeared a naïve simpleton to the bishop ever since their days as students together. So it had proved yet again. Surely, he must have seen the signs of rising support for other faiths. Father Sage had always clung to outdated and redundant forms of thought and worship. It had come to Bishop Gibot's notice from several sources that Father Sage was still against the ordination of women priests and against the acceptance of homosexuality and gay marriage. Furthermore, the local deacon had confirmed for the bishop that Father Sage had been preaching that the Christian faith was too tolerant of criticism when compared to other faiths. It appeared that Father Sage had advocated asserting fundamental Christian beliefs such as the resurrection of Christ and the virgin birth. *What piffle,* the bishop had thought. *How can we move forwards with our brothers in faith if we cling to these ancient and metaphorical myths which have caused so much dissent and schism in ignorant past centuries?*

It was not rocket science to sift the metaphorical from the literal in ancient texts. These texts were written by relatively ignorant, uneducated barbarians after all. Why did so many of his colleagues make such a fuss out of trivial and obvious details? And the transgender sermon from Father Sage was a final problem which just sealed his fate and made it so much easier to oust him.

"Well, well, thank you so much for coming to see me today, Father," purred the bishop. "I will show you to the door and let you get on with planning your exciting future. Are you planning anything stimulating this weekend?"

The heavy oak door of the bishop's lodge swung slowly closed behind Father Sage. In a daze, Father Sage walked slowly down the gravel drive between the beautifully maintained laurel, holly, and rhododendron bushes to his car. He pondered what his future held. He felt numb with shock at the bad news. At least the bishop was offering a good reference. With some application and patience, surely a position would be forthcoming soon.

Alone again in his study, the bishop lifted the telephone receiver and dialled.

"Hello, Charles. Yes, very well, thank you. No, the reason I am phoning is about a priest who is leaving my diocese in the next month. Not a great success, I am afraid. One of these rather rigid bigoted types who cannot cope with the improvements we have all embraced in recent decades. Yes, you know the sort. Name? Sage—Father Joseph Sage. Just in case he contacts you for a post. All enquiries to be passed to me, and I will write any reference personally. Not something I could put in writing, of course. You understand. Very good. All the best to Andrea. Speak soon."

Half an hour and several more telephone calls later, the bishop poured himself a small sweet sherry and sat staring into the beautifully tended garden of the bishop's lodge. Even if there had been suitable posts, Bishop Gibot was determined that Father Sage would not work within the church in any capacity at any time in the future. It was always regrettable when a priest did not fit into the prevailing philosophy of the times.

Father Sage was a charming and pleasant chap. Indeed, he received glowing tributes from his parishioners, much to the surprise and consternation of the bishop. Also surprising was that numbers were rising in the cathedral chaplaincy attached to the university. However, this inconvenient truth was not allowed to interfere with the important task of removing priests who did not fit with the move towards a more diverse, inclusive, and eclectic faith community. Those who could not or would not support the ordination of women, closer links with Muslim, Jewish, and Hindu colleagues, and the inclusion of all genders and all sexual preferences would have to find another calling and another paymaster.

The bishop was particularly satisfied that he would be able to fund the cost of employing a religious liaison assistant by saving Father Sage's stipend—and with a net saving of several thousand pounds. It warmed his heart to think of the approving articles in the local ecumenical press when the liaison assistant had attended a blessing on the previous Sunday, wearing the full splendid niqab and burqa. The white of the bishop's cassock had contrasted beautifully with the deep black of the Muslim garb. Some of the more ignorant traditionalists in his diocese had muttered and spluttered at this innovation. Bishop Gibot had no concerns about this. Had not the archbishop himself praised and espoused sharia law? Bishop Gibot was certain that he was swimming in the mainstream current of ecumenical religious evolution towards the very highest office. *What a future lies before me*, he thought to himself.

Thinking further about this wonderful event, the bishop hoped somewhat doubtfully that it had really been the liaison assistant attending the blessing. One could never be sure with the full niqab and burqa, of course. However, it mattered little since the symbolism of the event and the prestige acquired by the bishop in the eyes of those with power within the Church were all important. The very thought of asking the liaison assistant to lift her veil to confirm her identity would have been ridiculous, of course. It would have been demeaning to her and below his dignity to ask. He shuddered at the thought.

The bishop's thoughts strayed further into the strategic planning which he had been building patiently for decades. It had been clear to Bishop Gibot that bottoms on seats and money in the collection box were the only real measures of success for a modern church. Very early in his career, it had become apparent that Islam and other branches of Christianity were infinitely more aware of this and far more commercially successful by this recruitment yardstick.

In the bishop's view, the church was doomed to a relentless and inevitable decline into irrelevance unless something radical changed. For Bishop Gibot, what needed to change was the linkage with more commercially successful faith systems. Surely, the bishop had concluded at an early stage of his career, a reunion of Christian faiths and then a union with other, more dynamic Abrahamic faith systems was the obvious way forward. For Bishop Leonard, an amalgamation of all faith systems stemming from the Abrahamic tradition was a delicious thought. In the secret recesses of his ambitious mind, he foresaw a glowing and very senior role for himself in the great new world of unified monotheistic religious faiths.

How interesting it is, thought the bishop, *that I, as a Christian leader, could help with multicultural understanding in such a wonderful way.*

A tiny speck of doubt crept into the bishop's mind. It would not be widely understood in conservative senior church circles—or in the conservative lay press—if it were known that a Christian bishop had funded a Muslim religious liaison assistant using funds donated by Christian parishioners by dismissing a priest with very traditional Christian views at this early stage of religious revolution. However, the bishop was able to dismiss these negative thoughts. It was inconceivable that the significant minority Muslim community in his diocese would object to this act of communion between faiths. The labyrinthine finances of the church were also far too obscure to permit public scrutiny of church finances. Bishop Gibot was certain that he would never be held accountable for this action. A very satisfactory situation, indeed. A smile played around his lips at the thoughts flitting across his mind.

Two hours later, Father Sage met with his sister, Karen, in a small coffee shop close to their family home. Karen Sage had worked as a solicitor for many years with a particular interest in employment law. She had never had to advise an Anglican priest about his employment rights before. Her brother's request had come as a surprise to her, so she had researched the law relating to Anglican priests.

"I understand your dilemma, Joseph," said Karen. "But unfortunately I don't think you have any remedy in law."

"How can this be, Karen?" replied Father Sage. "The bishop is effectively making me redundant without paying any redundancy compensation. And while my post still exists, it will probably be filled already by someone less qualified but more politically correct. Surely I have the same legal rights as everyone else?"

"My understanding is that there is a longstanding principle—indeed, it is an ancient legal principle—dating back over eight centuries to the time of the Magna Carta that priests are not employees or workers. They are called 'post holders.' As such, they have no legal employment rights. From my reading, I discovered that this was confirmed recently in an Appeal Court ruling," replied Karen.

"As a post holder, you have no rights of unfair or constructive dismissal and no rights to redundancy compensation. This is covered by ancient ecclesiastical law and not by secular law. I have looked this up, and it dates back to the law surrounding clergy appointments as far back as the Investiture Contest between the popes and the holy Roman emperors in the eleventh century and continuing right up to the introduction of common tenure in the ecclesiastical offices."

Father Sage stared out of the coffee shop window. His sense of outrage was acute. To be dismissed out of hand by a bishop such as Leonard Gibot, who had no values or principles, felt intolerable. He found it very difficult to think Christian thoughts about his own bishop at such a challenging time.

"So my best option is just to accept this dismissal and look for an alternative career. Is that what you are saying?" asked Joseph.

"Well, you could try to fight this legally in an employment tribunal, but you would have to overturn centuries of legal precedent. It would probably cost a fortune and take many years. You are fighting a very wealthy church who cannot afford to lose this principle, Joseph. Sometimes it is better to accept the inevitable and make the best of a difficult situation," replied Karen, reaching over to pat his arm.

Adila Barzin and her husband were both refugees from Afghanistan. They lived in social housing provided by British taxpayers on the outskirts of the cathedral city in England where Bishop Gibot held sway. Their home was provided by the British government for the settlement of asylum seekers.

In Afghanistan, she and her husband had been trained intensively for a very important project. Their professional background was in the nuclear energy industry in Pakistan before moving to Afghanistan. Both of them had different names and indeed completely different identities before seeking asylum in England.

Once she arrived in England, Ms Barzin sought employment at several Christian cathedrals in several large British cities. She was eventually successful in her application for the post of religious liaison assistant offered by Bishop Gibot at the Metropolitan Cathedral of Christ the King.

As soon as she was appointed to this post, she and her husband contacted a team of colleagues dispersed throughout the city. They were all prepared for this opportunity. On the first weekend after her appointment, early on a Saturday morning, while the administration offices of the cathedral were relatively quiet, a team of four people dressed in the full burqa, with the niqab face veil, drove a white minivan into the underground car park beneath the cathedral. The car park was almost deserted at this time.

The four "females" unloaded numerous unlabelled boxes and several pieces of equipment into a storage office which had been allocated to Mr Barzin. They spent almost the entire weekend coming and going, working on the equipment they had unloaded. While there was CCTV outside the cathedral, the underground car park was not fully covered by CCTV, and there were blind spots. Security

staff at the cathedral are relatively relaxed at the best
of times. On this particular weekend, they were unconcerned by the comings and goings. They knew of
Ms Barzin's appointment, and they were expecting
some Muslim staff to be in and out while Ms Barzin
set up her team. They were very impressed with the
work ethic of their new colleagues, who seemed to
be working for most of the day and night.

Back at their family home at the end of the weekend, Mr Barzin turned to her husband.

"Preparations for our celebration are complete,"
she said with a broad smile on her face.

"God is great," Mr Barzin replied with an equally
broad smile.

CHAPTER 9

INTERVIEW

British Army report states that using words such as "patriot" and "Islamofascism" is a sign of right-wing extremism. Action recommended against any soldier who "demonstrates negative opinions" about politically correct army recruitment videos.
—*Mail Online*, 2017

Father Sage's record in interviews of the past weeks had been poor or possibly even disastrous. Ten applications, five interviews, and five rejections so far since he was informed that his current post was being terminated. Today was going to be very different, he hoped.

"And what special characteristics would you bring to the post at St Luke's, Father Sage? Why should we pick you before any of the other candidates?" The chairman of the interview panel intoned his questions in a drone.

Clearly, this interview panel is just going through the motions, thought Father Sage. His sixth interview since the bishop had given him notice to quit was not going particularly well. The body language of the panel suggested boredom and disinterest.

"My views are traditional, as you know, sir," answered Father Sage. "I support the work of women in the church but not the ordination of women priests or bishops. I cannot support gay marriage. My view is that scripture tells us that marriage is between a man and a woman. I have struggled with the baptism and marriage of those who demonstrate no religious faith. I have a desire for dialogue with those of other faiths, but I value also the distinct and unique Christian message of our church above all else. I feel that the church often fails to deliver a clear Christian message these days. Our message seems diluted by political correctness and fear of offending minority interest groups. I do not support the idea of endorsing sharia. I hope I can provide spiritual guidance for your parish in a manner which is both relevant for our times but also rooted in traditional Christian values."

"And precisely what basis in scripture do you have for your view that women should not be ordained?"

the deputy chairwoman shot back while glancing at her fellow interviewers. Her severe short-back-and-sides haircut and dark blue business suit with trousers emphasised her unisex clothing preferences. Father Sage felt that an honest answer from him would be the end of his application for this post, but he launched into it anyway. *Honesty is the best policy,* he thought to himself.

"I believe there are three general scriptural foundations for the male-only priesthood," replied Father Sage. This was a well-rehearsed topic for him. Inwardly he groaned because he knew these honest views would disqualify him from the post in the eyes of this questioner. "Firstly, I believe that Leviticus 6–8 restricts participation in sacred rites to males— specifically, 'to Aaron the priest and to his *sons,* as a perpetual due from the people of Israel...throughout their generations.' Christ did not annul this practice, of course.

"Secondly, there are numerous references to priests being 'Father' to their flock, not 'Mother,' starting with Abraham in Genesis, then Matthew, Luke, John, and Acts. Finally, of course, Christ himself chose men only as his apostles. The washing of the feet of the disciples by Christ is considered a preparatory purification for their assimilation into his eternal priesthood. This was an ordination ceremony that ended on the evening of Easter Sunday, when our Lord empowered his Apostles—all men—to forgive sins, as we see in John 20:21."

Father Sage seemed keen to continue with more detailed scriptural arguments, but the interview panel was starting to fidget restlessly in the face of this onslaught of scriptural knowledge and argument. They had clearly not expected such accurate or literal quotation of scripture. Some of them appeared indifferent or antagonistic to this line of argument.

"Surely you cannot claim that we are bound by Bronze Age and first-century writings in a literal manner," interrupted the chairman. "The church must adapt to our times. This is what Christ did during his lifetime by adapting the Old Testament teachings to his contemporary context." The chairman paused and there was an uncomfortable silence. Father Sage could see that his answer was not being received in a positive way by the interview panel. He groaned inwardly. He knew this was a sixth rejection in the making.

"You might be aware that we have a respite centre for the care of the terminally ill in our parish, Father," suggested the interview chairman. "What experience do you have ministering to the dying?" This was clearly an attempt to divert the dialogue onto less contentious territory.

"I have been chaplain to the Royal Victoria Infirmary for several years," replied Father Sage. "In cooperation with colleagues from other faiths, I have been offering spiritual guidance to those who call me to the hospital. I feel this will be a helpful and positive background for work at the respite centre."

Ten minutes later, Father Sage was sitting in his car, a red Mini Cooper with a Union Jack painted on the roof, preparing to drive away from St Luke's. It was a very tight squeeze for a man of middle age and fond of his chocolate snacks. A sharp rap on his window caused him to jump. He wound the window down.

"Father, I just wanted to thank you for coming." It was the parish treasurer. Father Sage had always got on well with the treasurer when helping out with services during the local vicar's annual leave. "I was plugging hard for you. However, our chairman is stubborn and had his mind set on Diane Payne. No official decision yet, of course, but I can see the writing on the wall. Between you and me, in strictest confidence, Bishop Gibot has been blackballing you. If I were you, I would try to get a reference from your previous bishop. I know this could look odd, but you are stuffed if Leonard Gibot has anything to do with your interviews.

"Also, just a tip about Lyndsey Joel, who is responsible for our discrimination policies. I understand from the grapevine that she raised the complaint about your sermon which covered gender and transgender issues herself. It seems that none of your parishioners objected at all. It was only Ms Joel who decided to raise the complaint and then to deal with the complaint herself. A bit of a conflict of interest, of course. However, she is a rather powerful figure in the current PC climate. Many people are rather scared of her, and few dare to challenge her. She chairs the local branch of the Campaign for Eradication of Masculine Toxicity—CAMERAMAT, as you probably know."

This was very disappointing but not entirely surprising to Father Sage. This parish was a traditional area which had never had a female priest. It seemed that someone had stitched it up for Diane Payne to get the post even before the interview. How could a middle-aged, white, male, traditional priest survive in these days of political correctness and antimale, antiwhite prejudice?

"Many thanks, David. I think we should rename it the Campaign for Eradication of Men—CAMERAMEN. I know when I am beaten, especially by the better 'man.'" Father Sage hoped this did not sound too bitter.

Driving back to his flat, Father Sage pondered his fate. Why would Bishop Gibot be so petty and difficult about this move? *First he pretends to scrap the chaplaincy post, and now he actively blackballs me. Shoddy goings-on. Call the man a Christian? He certainly doesn't seem to care about priests under his episcopal care*, thought Father Sage.

CHAPTER 10

DISCOVERY

B ishop Gibot walked slowly round the circular cathedral nave. The cathedral was almost empty. It
was midafternoon, and there was no mass scheduled
for several hours. He was on his way to check on the
newly recruited religious liaison officer.

He descended the spiral staircase to the crypt
and headed for the administration offices. As he
turned into the administration corridor, he noticed
some small cameras mounted at the corner of the
corridor pointing in both directions. *These must be
new*, he thought. *I have definitely not noticed these before.
The security team must be beefing up security. I wonder
why.*

He approached the office of Adila Barzin and
knocked on the door. There was no answer. He tried
the door handle. The door opened. It was dark inside, so the bishop leaned in through the door and
switched on the light. The office was full of storage

boxes apart from some complex-looking electronic machinery on the far wall. Lights were blinking from various metallic pieces of machinery, and the images of empty corridors appeared on several computer screens. *Strange,* he thought, *that Ms Barzin's office should be full of this equipment.* It all looked very modern and sophisticated.

Someone opened the door to the next office. A figure dressed in the full burqa and full veil stepped out of the office and looked towards the bishop.

"Can I help you?" the veiled figure asked while approaching the open door, gently pushing the bishop aside, switching off the light and closing the door firmly.

"I am Bishop Gibot," replied the bishop. "I am looking for Ms Barzin, the religious liaison assistant, for a quick chat. Do you know where she is by any chance?"

Immediately, a second figure, also dressed in the full burqa with veiled face, stepped out of the same office door as the first veiled figure and spoke.

"Good afternoon, Bishop. So nice to see you. Please come in." The voice from the veiled figure clearly belonged to Adila Barzin. She guided and ushered the bishop hastily into the open office. The bishop noticed the second veiled figure locking the office full of boxes and equipment as he was encouraged into the next-door office. A handful of people, all of whom were dressed in burqas with veiled faces, were in the office he entered. Adila spoke rapidly in Arabic, and all of these people exited the room without speaking, leaving the bishop alone with Ms Barzin.

"I apologise, Bishop," explained Ms Barzin. "I have reorganised my offices. The storage room has been moved to my original office. That was the office you were knocking at, which I have locked. This is now my office." Mr Barzin indicated the room they were standing in.

"I see. Excellent. Good to see you are getting stuck into things," muttered the bishop. "Just out of interest, what exactly are you storing in the next office?"

"Oh, nothing important," replied Ms Barzin. "Just information leaflets, material for meetings, and a couple of computers, really. Everything is going very well. My team members have already reached out to several religious leaders in the city. We have had a very warm reception."

"Jolly good," commented the bishop. "Is there anything you need? Are we giving you all you require?"

"Absolutely. We have everything in place," replied Ms Barzin.

"Righty ho. I will leave you to it, then," said the bishop. He left Ms Barzin and walked back along the administration corridor towards his office.

There was no sign of the other people who had exited Ms Barzin's new office as the bishop walked towards his office. *Why would she need all that machinery in the new storage room for a liaison role?* the bishop thought briefly before moving onto more pressing thoughts.

Once the bishop was out of sight, Adila Barzin called her colleagues back into her office.

"The bishop saw inside the storage room. Our position is vulnerable, especially since the loss of our backup supplies in the fire," said one figure with a deep male voice behind his veil.

Ms Barzin replied in Arabic. At times the veiled figures engages in heated discussions. The bishop's visit had clearly caused some concern amongst Ms Barzin's small group.

CHAPTER 11

DEATH

The crypt in the cathedral was originally designed by Sir Edward Lutyens in 1929. Work on the design by Lutyens for the cathedral began in 1933 but was stopped at the crypt stage by the bombing of the city during the Second World War. The Nazis were trying to destroy freedom across Europe. In the end, they only delayed the construction of the cathedral by a few years.

The crypt now contained a tomb which had a pierced round stone door, known locally as the "rolling stone," which rolled into place to close the tomb. The controls for the round door lock were outside of the tomb with interlock systems to prevent anyone from accidentally locking themselves in the tomb. The tomb was faced with polished granite. The modern cathedral was built on top of the traditional Lutyens crypt in contrasting stark concrete, glass, and steel between 1962 and 1967 using a later design by Frederick Gibberd. It was affectionately known as Paddy's Wigwam by the locals due to the unusual shape of the stained-glass windows in the beacon, which resembled a North American Indian wigwam.

Several weeks after the awkward meeting during which he had given Father Sage notice to leave his post, Bishop Gibot was sitting in his office in the cathedral considering his sermon for the afternoon mass. He was dressed in a resplendent cope of watered silk, embroidered in coloured silks and couched with metal thread. *How magnificent I am*, he thought to himself. *This is what I was born to do.*

A variety of thoughts were competing for his attention on this June morning. He felt calm and satisfied having completed the difficult task of dismissing a parish priest some weeks previously. He reflected that it was always sad when it became necessary to remove a priest from his calling. However, the demands of accountants and tax officers now stood high in the affairs of the church in the twenty-first century. It was no longer possible for a bishop in the church to ignore the reality of falling attendance, budget cuts, and income reductions, especially after the global credit crunch. Had this not been the case in biblical times? Had our Lord himself not instructed us to give unto Caesar that which is Caesar's?

So the accountants and tax collectors must be paid their due. After all, pensions cost money, especially the bishops' pensions. Earthly expenses were unavoidable even for a spiritual organisation. Foreign travel was a necessity, and bishops were expected to uphold the dignity of the church in the manner of their travel and accommodation during such journeys. Some would always complain of lavish excess in the church. This made it all the more important to be discreet about church generosity to faithful elder servants.

"Shall I prepare the communion wine, Your Grace?" asked George Peterson, the deacon of the Cathedral of Christ the King.

"Yes, yes. Many thanks, George. Please proceed. We will no doubt need extra for the larger congregation today," replied the bishop.

George Peterson had been a deacon at the cathedral for less than two years. After the suicide of his father many years previously, George had sought refuge and solace in the church. Eventually, the pain of losing his father had lessened. He knew he could never get over such a loss, but he gradually adapted to the hole in his life. He thought now about his father every day. This morning he tried to put negative thoughts out of his mind as he prepared for mass.

George moved to an adjoining room and careful-ly poured out the communion wine into the cruets, the glass decanter used for storing communion wine before a mass, and prepared the wafers. After twenty minutes the bishop called from the adjoining room. George carefully wiped the lip of the cruets and the surface of the oak table on which it stood.

"George, is this right?" asked the bishop, study-ing the leaflet for the service that afternoon. "Is Father Sage attending the mass today?"

"Oh, yes, Your Grace," replied George. "I con-firmed this morning with Father Sage since this will probably be his last week in your diocese. He will be assisting you."

"Most unfortunate," mused the bishop. He had hoped to avoid further meetings with Father Sage after dismissing him from his post.

"I'm so sorry, Your Grace—what was unfortu-nate?" asked George.

"No, nothing. I was just talking aloud. All will be well, I am sure," replied the bishop. "George, do you know where my medication is?"

George took a blister pack of capsules from a drawer, walked through to the bishop's office, and handed these to the bishop. The bishop's hands shook slightly as he pressed two capsules onto the oak table in front of him. He swallowed these with a mouthful of water. His head shook slowly as he replaced the blister pack in his jacket pocket and mopped his brow with a crisply folded white handkerchief.

Three hours later, Bishop Leonard Gibot stood at the altar in the magnificent Cathedral of Christ the King and lifted the chalice of communion wine slowly from the altar towards his lips. It was a very warm summer afternoon in the cathedral. A small bead of sweat glistened on his forehead. The mass was reaching its conclusion. The wine in the chalice smelled sweet but spicy. Bishop Leonard took a generous mouthful from the chalice and swallowed all of the remaining communion wine. He looked and felt healthy, but Bishop Gibot had less than an hour to live.

As he swallowed, Bishop Gibot registered a slightly different taste compared to the normal communion wine. As the ceremony progressed to its normal conclusion, he wondered what the bitter taste was. The congregation had been a little disappointing, and there had been a considerable amount of surplus communion wine. Bishop Gibot had consumed almost two full chalices. A slight feeling of nausea was beginning in the pit of his stomach and tingling in his jaw and shoulders. *The cathedral dais is very hot today*, he thought. As seconds passed, the nausea grew. *It is so hot today*, he thought. *I must get out of this cassock as soon as possible.* Sweat started pouring from his temples and brow. He felt his heart pounding rapidly in his temples. He recalled a similar feeling several years before with dread. As the cathedral started to spin in front of his eyes, he knew that something very serious was happening. He knew he must get away from the large and very public altar. He grabbed the candle stand to steady himself. The lit candle toppled to the floor and spluttered.

Father Sage was standing to one side to assist the bishop. He noticed the pallor on the bishop's face and the beads of sweat starting to glisten on his brow. He watched as the bishop turned to the deacon and stumbled.

"I am not feeling well," Bishop Gibot whispered to his assistant deacon, George Peterson. "I need to go somewhere cooler and quiet to rest." He paused and breathed deeply. "I need to go right now, George," he said with some urgency.

"Your Grace, let me help you. We can go to the crypt to rest," replied George. He turned to Father Sage while supporting the bishop. "Please, could you take over, Father Sage? The bishop is unwell. I will assist His Grace."

Mr Peterson led the bishop swiftly to the stairs, supporting his elbow, and guided him down the spiral stairs towards the cooler, darker crypt. Father

Sage automatically took over the ceremony to finish the mass without hesitation. Members of the congregation wondered what had happened to the bishop to require Father Sage to take over the mass.

As Bishop Gibot and Deacon Peterson walked slowly through the corridors of the crypt, lined by the cool brickwork laid by the original architect Lutyens in the nineteenth century, Bishop Gibot started to feel slightly less nauseous.

They passed the tomb of the rolling stone. The crypt was almost deserted. There was just one member of the public in the corridor as far as they could see.

"Why don't you rest in the tomb for a few minutes?" suggested Mr Peterson. "There is a seat inside. It is cool and quiet. You can catch your breath."

George Peterson supported the bishop through the large door to the tomb. The heavy circular door had been rolled aside to allow public access, which was normal during office hours. The bishop sat heavily on the stone seat in the tomb and breathed deeply.

"Leave me, George. I will be fine in a few minutes," ordered the bishop.

"I think I should call a doctor, Your Grace," George suggested, frowning with indecision.

"Leave me. I will be fine. Stop fussing, George. Now, get out." This was an order. The bishop waved his hand dismissively. George Peterson walked out of the tomb, hesitated at the door, then hurried along the corridor and up the spiral steps, glancing backwards frequently with a worried frown on his face.

Within a few seconds, the tightness in the bishop's chest started suddenly and came with a feeling of terror and a ringing in his ears. As he slipped from consciousness, he thought he saw a figure standing in the doorway to the tomb staring at him. He reached forwards and tried to call for help. No words came from his mouth. He was unable to speak. His last thoughts were a memory of similar sensations when he had suffered his heart attack years earlier. He slumped forwards onto to the floor of the tomb and rolled onto his back.

As he lay, unable to move, he sensed that the figure at the door of the tomb moved towards him. He could see shadows only, and a blurred face hovered in front of his eyes. He heard breathing and felt the breath of his visitor on his cheeks. The smell of sweet almonds came to him, and he wondered why this seemed important. He was unable to move or speak but wanted to shout for help. The figure hovering over him paused for what seemed a long time. The bishop's senses gradually faded to a black emptiness, and as this happened, the visitor seemed to move away smoothly towards the door of the tomb. Bishop Gibot's last sensation was hearing the door of the tomb roll slowly into place, locking his dying body in the tomb.

Less than five minutes later, a paramedic arrived with George Peterson at the tomb. A local doctor, Dr Neil Watson, accompanied them, having volunteered from the congregation when he saw the arrival of the paramedics. The paramedics were disturbed to find that the heavy circular stone door to the tomb was closed and locked. They could see the body of the bishop in the tomb through the pierced stone door, lying still on his back.

Because the heavy circular stone door to the tomb was closed and locked and because the interlock system prevented the general public from operating the mechanism, it was not possible to open the door without access to the door codes. Mr Peterson did not carry these codes with him. It took a further fifteen minutes for the crypt manager to be located and brought to the tomb and for the door to be opened. Members of the congregation attending mass were alerted by the commotion and followed the officials down into the crypt. Assistant priests and a group of parishioners jostled outside the tomb to investigate the fuss.

Dr Neil Watson had been in the congregation to observe mass and receive a blessing. Dr Watson had been in medical practice in a private clinic on nearby Hope Street and at a local hospital for several decades. He made frequent visits to the cathedral which was in effect his local chapel. He had introduced himself to the paramedics as they arrived and offered his professional services to assess and treat any casualties. Dr Watson and the paramedic rushed past the rolling door as it eventually moved slowly aside. Dr Watson knelt by the prostrate bishop.

"Bishop, can you hear me?" asked Dr Watson while shaking the bishop's shoulder gently.

There was no response from the bishop.

Dr Watson listened carefully for any sound of breathing and felt for a carotid pulse. He could not hear breathing or feel any pulse. He squeezed the bishop's hand hard. Still no response. He noticed that the bishop's skin felt very cold to the touch. Far colder than he would have expected for a person who was alert and conscious less than an hour previously. Dr Watson and the paramedics started cardiopulmonary resuscitation immediately.

After forty-five minutes of cardiopulmonary resuscitation with no heartbeat, Dr Watson asked the paramedics if they agreed that there was no point continuing to attempt resuscitation. The paramedics concurred, and they ceased any further attempt to pummel and shock Bishop Gibot's body back into life. The bishop was declared dead by Dr Watson. He lay in full view of hundreds of stunned parishioners by this time, eyes wide open, staring blankly towards the ceiling.

Father Sage, Deacon George Peterson, and Charles Lambert stood amongst the parishioners staring as the bishop's body moved past on a stretcher towards the exit, supervised by the paramedic and Dr Watson. Dr Watson looked at these three colleagues as he passed with the body and nodded in acknowledgement.

CHAPTER 12

INVESTIGATION

Father Joseph Sage agreed to meet Detective Inspector Everton at the main city police station. After the usual pleasantries, the detective launched into his questions.

"Thank you for agreeing to meet me, Father Sage. Can I ask if you knew Bishop Gibot well?" Inspector Everton started his line of questioning.

"Not very well, really," replied Father Sage. "We were at theological college together decades ago. We worked in the same diocese, of course, and officially he was the bishop with responsibility for my role. We had very little need to meet and very little in common. I rarely met the bishop."

"Do you know anyone who might have had a grudge against the bishop?"

"No. I don't think so, Inspector," replied Father Sage. *At least no more so than for any other hypocritical,*

153

disingenuous, faithless, dishonest twerp, thought Father Sage.

"I believe that you were recently given notice to quit your job with the church. Is that correct, Father?"

"Well, yes. I am sorry to say my post is not continuing. I am currently looking for another post," replied Father Sage.

"And it was the bishop's decision to fire you. Is that also correct, Father?"

"I suppose so. I mean, well, yes, it was his decision," replied Father Sage.

"Were you aware that Bishop Gibot was blocking your appointment to several other posts in the diocese?" asked the detective.

There was a long pause while Father Sage studiously looked away from Inspector Everton's gaze.

"I had heard rumours that Bishop Gibot was not my greatest fan," replied Father Sage hesitantly.

"Did you and the bishop argue about your dismissal at all?" asked the detective.

"Not really. I was relatively powerless due to the contractual role of ordained priests. I served at the bishop's pleasure. A bishop can dismiss a priest without compunction. Priests have no real employment rights. I accepted my situation and simply tried to find alternative employment," replied Father Sage.

Inspector Everton wrote a note of the latest answer in his notebook and then changed the subject slightly.

"Are you aware of any other clergy—or indeed anyone else in the church—in a similar situation in relation to the late Bishop Gibot?"

"In a similar situation? What exactly do you mean by that?" asked Father Sage.

"Well, do you know of anyone else who might have wanted to harm the bishop?" clarified the detective.

Father Sage thought carefully for a minute before replying. "The bishop was a man with a clear purpose and great ambition. He wanted to achieve many things in the church, and he was successful in most of his aims. The church is a conservative institution in which change is not welcomed by everyone. Of course, the bishop had opponents within the church. Did I know anyone who opposed Bishop Gibot? Yes, of course. Did I know of anyone who threatened him or wanted to harm him? Not at all. The church is a Christian institution, after all," replied Father Sage.

Father Sage was in the cathedral clearing up after a daily service in one of the side chapels. The sunlight was shining through the multicoloured stained-glass windows and casting a rainbow of colours over the chapel walls.

As he collected the hymn books, someone approached him.

"Excuse me. Are you Father Joseph Sage?" asked the stranger.

Joseph looked up. A middle-aged man in a rather worn suit with very short hair and lively, intelligent eyes was smiling at him.

"Yes, indeed. Joseph. How can I help you?"

"My name is Gerard Harrison. I work for *The Daily Post*. We want to run some articles as a tribute to the late Bishop Gibot. Would you mind giving us some background on the bishop?" asked the journalist.

"Well. Yes, of course. Let me clear these hymn books up, and we can find a spot to chat," replied Joseph.

Ten minutes later they retired to one of the small balconies which overlooked the cathedral nave. These were almost always empty and quiet on weekday afternoons.

"Fabulous cathedral," commented Gerard. "I don't come here very often, but when I do, I always find it inspirational. Calm and quiet. Good for thinking. Unless the organist is practising and then you get a free concert."

"I am glad you find some inspiration here," replied Joseph. "What would you like to know?"

"The bishop died suddenly in the tomb in the crypt, I understand. Was the bishop ill leading up to his death?"

"Not as far as I am aware," replied Joseph.

"There were rumours that Bishop Gibot liked to drink. Were you aware of this at all?"

"Well, now, we all like the occasional glass of wine, Gerard. The bishop was not teetotal."

This doesn't sound much like a tribute to me, thought Joseph.

"I understand that the bishop had recently appointed some liaison assistants who are Muslim. This has triggered some gossip around the city. Do you know of any resistance to a Christian bishop paying Muslims with money that Christians have donated to the church?"

Joseph considered how best to respond for a few seconds. "Of course, there were a few who might have raised an eyebrow at the new religious liaison assistant. However, this was a lay position, and the role did require someone who had an understanding of many religions. Equal opportunity for all, you know."

"But Father Sage, do you think it was right to divert money donated by Christians to pay those from another religion? I don't think the same would be true in reverse. Do you? Is this not a small example similar to the archbishop promoting sharia law? Are Christian leaders not abdicating their heritage in the name of political correctness?"

I think this chap has a point, thought Joseph.

"Well, there are several ways to look at this, I think. As with all things, it is important to consider various perspectives," Joseph said as ambiguously as he could manage.

"Mmm. I see," responded Gerard. "Father Sage, you work as the chaplain attached to the university and the cathedral, don't you?"

"That's right, Gerard. A very interesting role. Plenty of sceptical students and enthusiastic tourists. Lots to do always," Joseph said.

"And your post has been axed during recent cost savings. That is also the case, I think? What are your plans now?" asked Gerard.

"Oh, I am looking for a similar post elsewhere. I am sure something will turn up," replied Joseph.

"You caused a stir with a sermon about gender pronouns, I understand. Was this popular with church leaders?" asked Gerard as innocently as he could.

"Well, it caught their attention certainly," Joseph said.

"And are you permitted freedom to draft your own sermons, or does someone have to approve your words?" Gerard had heard some rumours about this.

"The bishop and I had a robust exchange of views, and I made it clear that priests must be free to speak out if we see injustice or unfairness," responded Joseph.

"And will you appoint a Muslim liaison assistant when you get another post, Father?"

Joseph smiled at this question. The two men looked at each other and exchanged a silent understanding.

Detective Inspector Malcolm Everton led George Peterson into the interview room at the city police headquarters. The building was deteriorating rapidly and needed much renovation. The paintwork had not been refreshed for many years, as was the case for most British police stations. Inspector Everton offered Mr Peterson a drink of water, and they sat opposite each other. The cheap metal chairs scraped on the concrete floors, and the sound echoed noisily in the drab interview room.

"Firstly, let me thank you for agreeing to meet me to clarify some details about the death of Bishop

Gibot," explained the detective. "I hope to clear up the remaining points fairly quickly."

"Of course, Inspector," replied Mr Peterson. "I am very happy to help in any way I can."

Inspector Everton thumbed through his notebook and then read some sections from a folder of papers he spread on the table between them.

"Can you confirm your relationship with Bishop Gibot?" asked the detective after a pause of several minutes.

"I serve as the deacon of the Metropolitan Cathedral of Christ the King. As such, I serve to support Bishop Gibot. That is, I served the bishop before he died, of course," said Mr Peterson.

"Now, you mentioned in your original written statement that the door to the tomb was still open when you left the bishop to summon emergency medical help. Is that correct?" asked the detective.

"Yes, indeed, Inspector. The stone door to the tomb is very heavy and is operated electronically. It cannot be closed by hand. The controls for the door lock are outside the tomb, and there is a security code. When he became ill, I left the bishop sitting in the tomb, but the door was wide open. I ran to obtain medical help. There was no need to close the tomb door. It would have wasted time and prevented speedy access for the paramedics," replied Mr Peterson.

"But the door to the tomb was closed when you returned with Dr Watson and the paramedic. Is that also correct?" asked the detective.

"Yes, sir. It took several minutes to get the door open again, which was very frustrating. Even though the bishop was lying on the floor by the time we arrived back, it is possible that the time wasted could have been critical."

"Can you explain how the door to the tomb came to be closed if you left it open and if the bishop was too ill to stand and remained inside the tomb?" asked Inspector Everton.

"I am afraid I have no idea how this occurred, Inspector. Someone must have closed and locked the door from the outside. The door cannot be locked from inside the tomb. However, as far as I recall, there was nobody in the crypt, or even near the crypt, when I left the bishop to summon help, and there was nobody in sight when I returned to the crypt with Dr Watson and the paramedic several minutes later. The bishop could have closed but not locked the door from inside the tomb, and in any case, as you say, he was unable to stand or walk when I left him," replied Mr Peterson.

"Am I right in thinking that your father also knew Bishop Gibot, Mr Peterson?" the detective asked.

George Peterson paused and a slight frown appeared on his face. This was an unusual change of subject which he had not expected.

"Well, yes. My father was the bursar of Selchester College when I was young. I believe that they knew each other during Bishop Gibot's training years at that college," responded Mr Peterson.

"And your father committed suicide sometime after Bishop Gibot graduated, I believe. Is this correct?" asked DI Everton.

Again a pause. George Peterson looked at the ceiling for a few seconds, exhaled slowly, and then replied. "Yes. My father did commit suicide."

"Was your father on good terms with Bishop Gibot before he died?" DI Everton posed this question while referring to his notes.

"I believe that my father had resigned as bursar several months before his death. I was an infant at the time, of course, so I knew nothing of these matters until adulthood. I learned the details from my mother. As far as I am aware, Bishop Gibot and my father were not in contact after my father resigned, but I have no way of knowing for sure, of course. I get the feeling that you already know the answers to these questions, DI Everton. Why is this relevant to the bishop's death?" asked Mr Peterson.

Everton ignored this question and continued to probe.

"Do you know why your father resigned from his post as bursar of Selchester College, Mr Peterson?" asked the detective.

"I am afraid I have no idea. Is this really relevant to the death of Bishop Gibot?" Mr Peterson moved restlessly in his chair.

"Let me enlighten you, Mr Peterson. Your father resigned because he was asked to resign by the college principal. The reason he was asked to resign was that there were allegations from several people in the town that he had…propositioned young men. At that time, such activity was illegal, of course. There were also allegations of assault on young men. The college paid significant sums to several local families to avoid a public scandal and costly legal cases. The price for your father was that he was asked to resign in return for avoiding prosecution and possible conviction for his alleged crimes."

Inspector Everton paused and looked up from his notes to examine the puzzled expression on George Peterson's face.

"And in his suicide note, your father wrote that one of the reasons he had decided to take his life was the fact that someone was blackmailing him for money even after he resigned. It appeared that someone at the college had knowledge of these allegations and had decided to take advantage of your father at a vulnerable time. So, you see, Mr Peterson, this context suggests that someone in your family may have had good reason to harbour ill feeling towards someone who was blackmailing your father at that time, just before his suicide. Were you aware of this, and do you know who might have been the blackmailer?" DI Everton asked in a flat monotone.

"I have no idea what you are talking about. I think this line of questioning is most impertinent. If you wish to continue with these questions, I feel that I should have legal representation. Now, unless there is anything further, I will bid you good day," George Peterson replied brusquely, stood from his seated position, and walked to the door.

"You are free to leave, of course, Mr Peterson. However, I may have further questions, and if so, you are free to request that your solicitor is present at any future interview," replied Inspector Everton as Mr Peterson left the room.

It was difficult for Gerard Harrison to find George Peterson. Journalists are usually good at finding people. Mr Harrison was quite good at evading contact.

Eventually Gerard managed to spot George Peterson leaving his office for the commute home one afternoon. Gerard walked up to the deacon and matched their walking speed.

"Mr Peterson, I am Gerard Harrison from *The Daily Post.* I am very sorry to bother you, but I am running a tribute to the late Bishop Gibot. Might we talk?" asked Gerard.

George Peterson tensed and started to walk slightly faster.

"Mr Peterson, I am aware that your father knew Bishop Gibot. It would be good if our tribute could honour your father's memory too," suggested Gerard.

That got his attention, thought Gerard. George Peterson stopped in midstride.

"Let me treat you to a coffee," Gerard said. He pointed George in the direction of a convenient Costa branch.

Sitting in the coffee shop with hot coffee in front of them, Gerard tried again. "Thank you so much for talking to me, Mr Peterson. It would be very helpful if you could flesh out the details of the bishop's character for me."

"Well, Bishop Gibot was a very energetic reformer within the church," started George.

"I have heard this about him," agreed Gerard. "And were you a supporter of his reforms?"

"Yes and no. The church always needs to maintain a contemporary feel—while adhering to our heritage and core principles, of course," replied George.

"Did your father know the bishop well?" Gerard moved the topic back in time.

"I cannot really say. I was too young at the time to really be aware," confirmed George.

"I understand that your father died tragically when you were young. I was sorry to read about this. It must have been a very hard time for your family."

George paused. "Yes...a terrible time" was all he managed.

"And the police never found out who was blackmailing your father, I think?" Gerard pushed harder.

"Sadly, no," replied George.

"How was the bishop's health in the past year?" Gerard directed the conversation elsewhere.

"Well, he had a heart condition, but he was taking regular medication, and it rarely seemed to trouble him," replied George.

"When he took ill on the day he died, you were kind enough to help him find somewhere to rest, I understand," probed Gerard.

"Yes, we managed to get to the crypt, and the bishop sat in the tomb while I went for help," confirmed George.

"But someone locked the tomb door—the large round stone door—and prevented help getting to him quickly enough. Isn't that right?"

"Yes. It is a real puzzle. There might have been someone else in the crypt at the time, but nobody saw who it was. In any case, the medics confirmed that it would have made little difference," George pushed back.

After ten minutes of further discussion, Gerard was unable to extract any more information of importance. He thanked George for his help, and they went their separate ways.

Detective Inspector Everton walked up to the medical consulting rooms on Hope Street. This was the part of the city that housed most of the private medical consulting rooms. The properties were large Victorian terraced houses. They had been built as townhouses for wealthy maritime merchants during the time of maximum British imperial world power in the nineteenth century. The merchants had long since left this part of town, and doctors and lawyers in private practice used the buildings for their lucrative private work. Everton examined the brass plate next to the wide hardwood door announcing; "Dr Neil Watson, MB, BCh, MRCP, Consultant Physician."

DI Everton was shown into Dr Watson's consulting room by the receptionist.

"Please take a seat, Inspector. Can I offer you a drink?" asked Dr Watson.

"No, thank you, Doctor. I just need a few minutes of your time to ask about the bishop's death last week if you don't mind," replied the detective.

"Of course. Ask away," suggested the doctor.

"I understand that you assisted in the efforts to resuscitate the late Bishop Gibot?" opened Everton.

"Indeed. Very sad that we were unsuccessful," replied Dr Watson.

"How exactly did you learn that Bishop Gibot needed medical assistance?" asked the Inspector.

"Mr Peterson came running to the reception staff in the cathedral lobby and asked them to telephone for emergency medical assistance for the bishop in the crypt. I overheard the conversation. I was in the congregation that day. I offered my services immediately, of course, as is my obligation in medical emergencies," replied Dr Watson.

"Who went to the crypt with you?" asked the Inspector.

"Actually, I went to the crypt on my own at first. Mr Peterson waited in the lobby of the cathedral for the arrival of paramedics. The paramedics and Mr Peterson joined me within a couple of minutes in the crypt," replied Dr Watson.

"When you arrived in the crypt, did you notice anything unusual?" asked the detective.

"Unusual. No, I don't recall anything in particular. What specifically are you getting at?" asked the doctor.

"Well, was the door to the tomb open or closed?" asked the detective.

"Oh, I see. Yes, of course. The door to the tomb was closed and locked when I arrived. I was trying to figure out how to open it when I was joined by Mr Peterson and the paramedics—and indeed a host of other members of the public," responded Dr Watson.

"And did you notice anyone near the tomb when you first arrived there?" asked the Inspector.

"Now that you ask, I think there might have been a figure standing a little away from the tomb when we arrived. An elderly man, I think, from memory. He looked a little scruffy, I remember. I recall thinking at the time that this was one of the locals who sleep rough on the streets in this area. It was unusual, though, because the tramps don't usually pay the fee to visit the crypt. They stay outside near the heating vents or they visit the refectory for a hot drink if they have loose change. They more commonly visit the mission café close by for a free meal if they run out of money. I don't think I saw this person again, and I did not recognise who it was. It was rather dark down there, of course, and we were all rather busy with the bishop's illness," replied Dr Watson.

"So you have no knowledge of how the tomb door came to be closed and locked?" asked the inspector.

"I am very sorry, Inspector. I have no idea how this happened," replied Dr Watson.

"Just on another topic," continued Malcolm, "you are a close friend of Father Sage. Is that correct?"

"Well, yes, we have been friends since senior school days. We see each other socially every week or two," replied Dr Watson.

"And you will be aware that Father Sage has been given notice to quit his job at the chaplaincy?"

"Yes, I was aware of this. However, I am sure that he will soon get another post," suggested the doctor.

"Are you aware of whether the bishop and Father Sage got on well?" asked the Malcolm.

"As far as I am aware, the bishop and Father Sage had a good working relationship," replied the doctor.

Apart from his racism, hypocrisy, gender prejudice, and almost complete lack of any ethical principles, the bishop was a great guy, thought Neil.

"Thank you, Doctor Watson. You have been very helpful," concluded Malcolm.

＊＝ ＝＊

Adila Barzin had only recently been appointed as the religious liaison assistant to Bishop Gibot. Adila was not Christian, of course. She had fled the turmoil in the Middle East and sought asylum in England. She had been surprised but delighted when Bishop Gibot had appointed her as the liaison assistant between their faiths. She was equally thankful to be allowed to wear the full veil during her working duties and to be invited to attend and observe religious ceremony in the cathedral while still wearing her veil. She had been given a couple of offices for herself and a few support workers in the cathedral administration suite.

Detective Inspector Everton met with Ms Barzin in her office in the cathedral complex. He attended with a female colleague.

"Ms Barzin, I am very grateful that you agreed to meet me. This is my colleague Detective Sergeant Wilson. I have a few questions relating to the bishop. I am sure this will not take much of your time," the detective said. "Could you outline your relationship with Bishop Gibot, please?"

"The bishop was my line manager. I have been employed for the past few weeks as a liaison assistant between the local mosques, other religions, and the bishopric. I did not know the bishop socially, and I never met him outside of work, Inspector."

"Am I right in thinking that there were some within the bishop's team who were not keen on the appointment of a Muslim to your post?" asked Inspector Everton.

"Well, I couldn't really say. Nobody said anything negative to me. Perhaps some might have preferred a Christian appointment. I am sorry—I cannot really help you with this question, Inspector," replied Adila.

"Are you aware of any of the bishop's colleagues who might have wanted to harm him or prevent him from pursuing his modernisation agenda?"

"Absolutely not, Inspector. As far as I know, all of our colleagues loved the bishop," replied Adila.

"One more thing, Ms Barzin. I was wondering why all of the people we see on this floor are in Muslim clothing?" asked Inspector Everton as a parting shot.

"These are just my assistants, Inspector," replied Ms Barzin. "I cannot do all of the work alone, and we need people fluent in English and Arabic."

Inspector Everton mentally ticked off Ms Barzin from his list of interviewees. All of her responses seemed plausible, and there were no contradictions. He thanked her, and both he and Sergeant Wilson left her office.

Ms Barzin waited for several minutes before picking up her mobile phone. She dialled an international number and listened to the dial tone for a while. When the call was answered, there was an initial period of silence before Adila spoke.

"Adila here. I have just finished the interview with the English police. It went as you predicted. The detective did not ask any questions about our friends who are preparing the gifts. He did not ask about either of the recent departures. He did not ask to inspect the storeroom and has not arranged any further appointments. It appears that it is safe to proceed as planned," said Adila.

There was another pause for several minutes, and then the line went dead.

Gerard Harrison approached Adila Barzin after she had attended one of the services at the cathedral. She was walking across the nave towards the lift which led to the administration offices.

"Excuse me, Ms Barzin, I am Gerard Harrison from *The Daily Post.* I wondered if you might have some comments for a tribute article we are running about the late Bishop Gibot?" asked Gerard.

Ms Barzin did not pause or stop walking. She continued towards the lift without a word.

"Ms Barzin, do you think that the local mosque would appoint a Christian as a liaison assistant?" Gerard tried while following Ms Barzin towards the lift.

The lift doors closed with Ms Barzin's eyes blazing at Gerard through the tiny gap in her veil.

Friendly lady with nothing to hide—not, thought Gerard.

A week after interviewing Ms Barzin, Detective Inspector Everton was meeting with the antiterrorism officer working in the city police force, Sergeant Mohammed Amin. Sergeant Amin, as his job title implied, was employed to help prevent terror-related incidents and to coordinate operational counterterrorism responses. "Prevent" was the title used for the government network of antiterrorist officers around Great Britain. Sergeant Mohammed Amin had been working in this post at Prevent for several years.

"Good afternoon, Mohammed," opened DI Everton. "Thank you for seeing me so soon. I just wanted to run through some developments in the case of Bishop Gibot."

"No problem, Malcolm. How can I help?" replied Sergeant Amin.

"Well, on the face of it, the evidence overall points to death by natural causes, possibly with some element of accidental adverse effects from prescribed medication. Bishop Gibot had a history of heart disease, and his lifestyle had not been particularly healthy for many years. Alcohol dependence had been a recurrent feature with the bishop. Several of his colleagues had reason to fall out with the bishop. A local priest had recently lost his job, and an administrator had some family history suggesting possible ill feeling. However, I doubt that either of these amount to much. The bishop was involved in a road traffic accident which resulted in a fatality many years ago, but again I doubt this is linked in any way to his death.

"There is a missing piece of the jigsaw in relation to the door to the tomb in which he died. The door was open when he was last seen alive, but it was closed and locked when the doctor and the paramedics arrived. It is not clear who closed and locked the tomb. The fact that it was locked delayed the paramedics for a few minutes, and this might have made all the difference. So far there is no evidence pointing to the person who locked the door," explained DI Everton.

"So why involve me? None of this suggests any terror-related activity. How can I help you?" asked Sergeant Amin.

"Right. Yes. I was getting to that." Inspector Everton marshalled his thoughts. "There is a liaison assistant who has only recently been appointed. Ms Barzin is her name. She is Muslim. She works between religious denominations to improve understanding and cooperation ostensibly. I interviewed her, and nothing of concern emerged. However, as a matter of routine, we have checked the telephone records of several of the key players in this matter. Ms Barzin made a single international call from her mobile phone shortly after I met with her. We don't know the content of the call. However, the number she phoned is on our list of suspected numbers related to the Paris attack on Charlie Hebdo in 2015.

I tried to arrange to meet Ms Barzin again to ask about this, and it turns out that she is nowhere to be found. Her colleagues don't know where she is. Some of them suggested she might be on leave. This seems implausible to me. Surely they would know this for sure. But the cathedral staff are in a bit of turmoil after the death of Bishop Gibot. I followed up her known address, and it appears that her passport and other documents were forged. She has effectively disappeared without a trace. I have no evidence to link her to Bishop Gibot's death directly. The only issue of concern is her telephone call and then her disappearance. It may simply be an immigration matter, of course."

"I can see your concern, Inspector," replied Sergeant Amin. "Okay, give me the details, and I will chase this up with my colleagues around the country and in INTERPOL."

"Another thing that has raised concern in the death of two other people in the city over in the past couple of months. One elderly man died in hospital, and one university professor died on holiday in Norway at almost the same time," continued the detective.

"So in what way are these other deaths linked to that of the bishop?" asked the sergeant.

"Well, the unusual feature of both of these other deaths is that they were both attributed to bone marrow damage of unknown cause. The very similar postmortem reports were cross-linked by the local coroner in the city, and he phoned me to alert me to this unusual coincidence quite separately. It turns out that both of these men were probably at the scene of a fire in the Irish Centre several weeks ago. Nobody was known to be injured in the fire, but Professor Mannheim was in the building with a priest when the fire started. They reported that there was an old man sleeping rough in there, but he disappeared.

"Both Professor Mannheim and the elderly man had probably been visiting that building regularly for a considerable period. Apparently bone marrow depression is a relatively rare condition, but it does occur occasionally, and usually no cause is found. In this case, two men suffered the same rare condition and died from it within days. The coroner informed me that one possible cause of bone marrow depression is high levels of radiation poisoning. Tests on the burned-out Irish Centre have detected some signs of radiation, but these are equivocal. The fire destroyed everything in the building, so it is hard to be sure what the source of radiation might be. This is the reason I contacted you. It is puzzling that any signs of radiation would be found in such a building, and the dose of ionising radiation required for this sort of illness is huge apparently."

"This is both puzzling and interesting," said Sergeant Amin. "Leave the file with me, and I will take this up with our radiation experts. Thank you for tipping me off, Malcolm. I'll get the file back to you as soon as possible."

Inspector Everton thanked his colleague and left the office.

Sergeant Amin walked to a filing cabinet, opened a drawer, and took out a small box. He opened the box, which contained twenty or thirty unused mobile phones still in their cases. He took out one phone, locked his office, and walked from the police headquarters down to the dockside area of the city.

He found a riverside seat away from the bustle of the tourists and shoppers and sat looking across the river. He inserted an unused SIM card into the new mobile phone and punched in a number. After several rings, someone answered the call. Without waiting for anyone to speak, Sergeant Amin spoke rapidly in Arabic for a few seconds. He ended the call, before anyone replied, removed the SIM card, and snapped it. He removed the battery from the phone, leaned over the railings, and dropped the broken SIM card, battery, and mobile phone in the river. All three disappeared into the murky brown sludge. He knew from past experience that this particular seat was shielded from CCTV cameras.

In a bedroom in Saudi Arabia, a young man was sitting at a computer desk wearing headphones. He listened carefully to a voicemail message. He then dialled a number in England from his keyboard. He spoke quickly in a dialect of Arabic when the call was answered. He then ended the call. He was confident that the call was not traceable because of the careful routing of the message via various friendly countries. The vulnerable state of British internet hardware was also helpful for him to conceal the nature, source, and content of his message.

In a terraced house on the outskirts of the cathedral city in England, Ms Barzin was relieved to receive a message. She turned to her colleague and delivered the message rapidly in Arabic. The room in which they were working was screened from the outside by plastic bags taped to the windows. There were several computer screens flickering on one wall and several workstations in the room. The images on the screens included CCTV monitoring the corridors and offices in the cathedral basement administration area. The people in the room displayed a calm efficiency.

CHAPTER 13

THE HOSPITAL

The Royal Victoria Hospital was a red-brick wonder in the nineteenth century when it was first built. The floors were tiled throughout and dormitory wards predominated. Clean tiles and open wards probably did more to protect the lives of patients than any surgeon or medication by making antiseptic cleaning simpler and easier. A century had taken its toll on the fabric of the building, and the tiles were now cracked, but it still served its population like an ancient soldier condemned to serve until death.

A new hospital was being built four hundred yards away. This new building was ten years behind schedule and hundreds of millions of pounds over budget. The new hospital wards included carpeted areas, which were a very good means of spreading infections between patients. Late in the building stage, the carpets were being ripped out and replaced with washable flooring. Nobody was made accountable for the gross financial mismanagement and waste of British tax pounds. Indeed, British taxpayers were largely unaware of these scandalous problems. The British worshipped their health service like a national religion. Freedom of speech was not encouraged by those with vested interests, such as health-care managers, health-care unions, and the biased British mainstream media, with respect to criticism of the British National Health Service.

Dr Neil Watson, consultant physician, was ensconced in his small office, a tiled Victorian room with high vaulted ceilings and huge windows overlooking the city and painted closed. One of the medical positions he held was that of chief medical officer at the infirmary. His duties included a visit to the hospital several days each week for routine administration and managerial tasks. Two piles of laboratory results and medical reports were peeking at him from his desk in an accusatory manner. *There is never enough time to complete everything fully*, he thought wistfully.

Slowly and methodically he picked up one result from the right-hand pile, considered the result, wrote a comment on the result and signed it, then placed it on the left-hand pile.

Dr Watson stared at the laboratory result for a few seconds. The result showed the postmortem findings for Bishop Leonard Gibot. Nothing surprising for the most part. Signs of coronary atheroma. Previous myocardial infarction confirmed with old scarring of the heart muscle. Signs of chronic alcoholic liver damage. *There was a known medical history of excess alcohol consumption, of course,* thought the doctor. No surprise there. Toxicology had picked up traces of a drug called disulfiram in the blood. *Now that's interesting,* thought Dr Watson. Preliminary findings were cardiac arrest due to longstanding myocardial ischemia. Dr Watson looked out of the window and considered carefully.

Bishop Gibot had been a patient at the hospital in the past. It was because of this that Dr Watson had seen Bishop Gibot as a patient before. Some of the bishop's past medical history was known to the doctor. Dr Watson folded the laboratory result and slotted it into his jacket pocket. He made a mental note to check more details about Bishop Gibot's medical history.

Two days later, the paper medical records for Bishop Gibot lay open in front of Dr Watson on his desk. Dr Watson read carefully, making selective notes on a blank sheet of paper. In 1985 the first signs of excessive alcohol consumption had been noted.

Detoxification treatment three times between 1985 and 1990. Road traffic accident in 1990 resulting in the death of a pedestrian and a drunk-driving prosecution. The case was dropped before trial on the grounds of ongoing detoxification treatment and lack of eyewitness evidence. An adverse reaction to Antabuse medication resulting in admission to hospital with chest pain. Clinical diagnosis of myocardial infarction at that time. Full functional recovery and then discharge with no serious loss of function. Most of this was known previously to Dr Watson.

The only puzzling part of this jigsaw was the toxicology from the postmortem. Why would Bishop Leonard take Antabuse again—or Disulfiram as it was also known—when he had suffered such a severe adverse reaction previously? The traces of Disulfiram found in the preliminary blood tests for Bishop Gibot were very low. They did not indicate that any significant amount of this drug had been consumed. However, there was no medical reason for Bishop Gibot to take this medication at all.

Could the bishop have accidentally taken some medication which contributed to his own death? Could a doctor have prescribed this without knowing the past history of a severe adverse reaction? *These are questions which might be hard to answer,* thought Dr Watson. *It may be too late, but I must ask that detective who interviewed me to make some more enquiries to confirm whether the bishop could have been taking this drug again.* He lifted the phone and dialled the number for Inspector Everton.

"Hello, Inspector. Doctor Watson here. I thought you might be interested in postmortem results on Bishop Gibot. Some blood tests have just come back. These relate to Bishop Gibot's medication. There was a miniscule trace of a drug called Disulfiram in one blood test. This is a drug used to treat alcohol dependence. Bishop Gibot had previously suffered a severe adverse reaction to this drug several years ago. This finding might be a spurious result, of course— a mistake by the lab. However, it occurs to me that it might be worthwhile finding out whether Bishop Gibot could have accidentally ingested Disulfiram. It may be the cause of his illness that day—and even the cause of his death. You will no doubt be examining his home where you might find evidence of medication taken. Also, if you have not yet done so, it might be worthwhile asking his family doctor if he had been prescribed this drug recently."

Doctor Watson paused to allow Inspector Everton to digest this information.

"Thank you very much for letting me know about this, Doctor Watson. I will certainly follow this up with the family doctor and check the bishop's home carefully," replied the inspector.

Dr Watson ended the call. *That should give the inspector a helpful line of enquiry and keep him busy for a while,* he thought to himself.

CHAPTER 14

DISCRIMINATION

An immigration policy which favours skilled, English-speaking people is racist.

—*United States Congresswoman*, 2019

Police in London investigate man who pretended to pray to Aladdin in Muslim prayer room as a blasphemy hate crime.

—*Breitbart Europe*, 2019

Gallery covers art works which depict Islamic script after complaints from Muslims that they are blasphemous.

—*The Times*, England, 2019

Professor claims Cambridge University discriminates against white, conservative men.

—*Daily Telegraph*, 2019

Detective Inspector Malcolm Everton took the lift to the top floor of police headquarters and walked down the thickly carpeted corridor to the office of Detective Chief Superintendent Clarissa Richards. Inspector Everton had never been to the top floor at police headquarters before. His invitation—or perhaps instruction—to attend a meeting had arrived without any explanation or notice.

"Detective Inspector Everton to see the chief superintendent," Malcolm reported to the personal assistant sitting outside the imposing hardwood double doors.

Inspector Everton was instructed to sit and wait, which he did. Half an hour later, Superintendent Richards opened her door and beckoned for Inspector Everton to enter.

"Have a seat, Malcolm. How are you finding things in the city centre?" asked the chief superintendent.

"Excellent, ma'am," reported Inspector Everton dutifully.

"Good. Good. Now you are probably wondering what this is all about," suggested the detective chief superintendent.

"Well, yes, I was wondering, ma'am," DI Everton said.

"This case you are looking into—the death of Bishop Gibot. Is it progressing?" asked Superintendent Richards.

"Yes. I think we are reasonably close to wrapping it up," replied Inspector Everton. "There is a development which needs to be tied up relating to two other deaths which might be related to accidental ionising radiation poisoning. There is also some discrepancy about the locked door of the tomb in which the bishop died. It is possible that the bishop may have accidentally taken medication which had an adverse effect. However, I don't think any of these lines of enquiry will delay us much longer. These are just loose ends which will be tied up soon."

"Indeed. That is good to hear. I am very pleased," said the chief superintendent. "The reason I invited you up for a little chat, Malcolm, is that there has been an informal complaint. The complainant wishes to remain anonymous, and the force would prefer this too. It appears that your enquiries touched on a Muslim lady who was working at the cathedral as a liaison assistant." The chief superintendent paused for a response.

"Yes, ma'am, that is correct. Ms Adila Barzin is the lady in question. I interviewed her simply as part of background information about the sudden death of the bishop. Ms Barzin did not have any useful information about the bishop's death. However, some unusual telephone traffic emerged shortly after our interview. I spoke to Sergeant Amin from the counterterrorism team. He is looking into the matter as we speak," replied Inspector Everton.

"I see. Thanks for confirming this, Malcolm. The informal complaint concerns Ms Barzin. It appears that she is worried that she has been singled out because of her religion or gender. Discrimination on the grounds of religion or gender is illegal, of course. Unless we have absolutely clear evidence to suspect Ms Barzin has committed some illegal act, it would be wise to act very carefully. The appearance of discrimination is not something that we would want to create, of course. Community relations in the city are pretty stable at present, and we want this to continue naturally," suggested the chief superintendent.

"The odd thing, ma'am, is that Ms Barzin seems to have disappeared. I was unable to contact her when I sought a follow-up interview, and she does not appear to have attended work for some time. With this in mind, it is odd that a complaint has been received. Has Ms Barzin contacted you directly?" asked Inspector Everton.

"Oh, no. Sorry, I didn't mean to mislead you. Ms Barzin has not contacted us. The complaint came from someone else. Someone who wishes to remain anonymous. The discrimination laws are very clear. We must avoid discrimination on grounds of gender or religion. We are not free to do or say whatever we wish if we risk discriminating on these grounds. We just want to ensure that this is kept informal and low key. So I hope you understand, Malcolm." The chief superintendent left her suggestion hanging rather ambiguously between them.

"Of course, ma'am. I will treat this matter with the greatest sensitivity," replied Inspector Everton.

"Very good. Unless there is a clear reason, I strongly suggest that we leave Ms Barzin alone. Perhaps you might run any further plans to interview her through my office," said the chief superintendent.

"Right, ma'am. If there is nothing else, I will crack on," suggested Inspector Everton, without actually committing to anything.

"Yes, of course, Malcolm. Thanks for coming up to see me. I look forward to a speedy conclusion of the bishop's case. Please keep me informed," the chief superintendent concluded.

Malcolm looked out of the window over the river as he walked back to his office on a lower floor. *What in heaven's name was all that about?* he wondered. *Ms Barzin has not complained and has disappeared, but some-one else has complained informally and anonymously.* The price of a false move might be career suicide in the politically correct days. *I had better tread very carefully with this investigation,* he thought. *Some of the bigwigs are taking a close interest. Not a good situation for an ambitious junior detective with current discrimination laws.*

Ms Barzin is most likely to have absconded due to irregularities in her immigration documentation, Inspector Everton thought. *My interview with her probably spooked her. What do I care about one more illegal immigrant?* Illegal immigration was so common in the current climate of mass immigration that it made any attempt to address the problem laughable. Bishop Gibot was an ill man past middle age with an unhealthy lifestyle, and he was probably taking the wrong medication. The fact that he had a few enemies was almost certainly immaterial. He considered that perhaps there was not really much point pursuing this case much longer as he entered his office.

On the fifth floor, Chief Superintendent Richards lifted her secure landline telephone and punched in a number. Sergeant Mohammed Amin answered almost immediately.

"Hello, Mohammed. Clarissa here. Just confirming I have spoken to Inspector Everton. I think I have persuaded him to leave Ms Barzin alone for now as you requested. I did not tell him about your counterterror investigations. I used another excuse. I am sure that he will stay away from this and there will be no risk of your operation being exposed. I hope this is helpful, Mohammed," confirmed the superintendent.

"Thank you, ma'am. I value your assistance. This is very helpful. I am sure this matter will reach a conclusion very soon," replied Sergeant Amin.

CHAPTER 15

THE FUNERAL

The funeral of Bishop Leonard Gibot was not well attended.

Father Joseph Sage sipped his tea slowly to avoid burning his mouth. Dr Neil Watson stood next to him. They both looked around the church hall. The assembled group of mourners were talking in subdued tones, standing in small groups.

"Why are we even here, Neil? Neither of us has ever a good word for Bishop Gibot," whispered Joseph.

"We are here because the old bastard is dead," replied Dr Watson. "And we deserve a moment to celebrate the fact that we will never have to put up with his insincere, manipulating, dishonest bullshit again. I have no hesitation in dwelling on this positive fact."

Charles Lambert walked through the double doors to the church hall, took off his wet coat, shook his wet umbrella onto the outer step, and wandered into the hall. His eyes picked out Neil and Joseph immediately, and he negotiated a path through the crowded hall towards them.

"Charles, how lovely to see you," said Father Sage. "Neil and I were just reflecting on our memories of the late bishop."

"Ah, yes. I can imagine the sort of memories you would be sharing," replied Charles.

"I suppose he must have had some redeeming features, but I cannot for the life of me bring any to mind," suggested Joseph.

"Indeed. Let's see. He was an alcoholic, probably guilty of murderer—at the least manslaughter—probably a blackmailer, and possibly an adulterer, *and* he worked hard to undermine the Christian values which he was sworn to uphold while at the same time promoting alternative religious ideologies that oppress women and advocate for burning blasphemous books and murdering people for their sexual preferences. What's not to like?" replied Charles.

The three men stood quietly for a few minutes contemplating the loss of their bishop and colleague, without any obvious regret.

"Watch out. I think our esteemed deacon has just arrived," said Joseph.

George Peterson walked into the church hall, folding his raincoat over his arm as he entered. His eyes quickly alighted on the group of three fans of the bishop. After collecting a cup of tea and a small biscuit, Mr Peterson made his way to join the three admirers.

"I am pleased to see you all," said Mr Peterson. "Despite the sombre nature of the occasion, I find within myself the capacity for some sense of relief. Even joy if I am honest."

"We all seem to be singing from the same hymn sheet today. If could use a religious simile," interjected Dr Watson.

There was another short pause, during which time the four men contemplated their sense of loss with smiles all around.

"Has anyone heard from the detective inspector recently?" asked Father Sage.

The other three men shook their heads in unison.

"I have no idea how the police investigation is going, but Inspector Everton seemed very interested in the door to the tomb being closed and locked from the outside," suggested Father Sage. "He was asking me about an old man who was spotted in the crypt at the time the bishop died."

"Yes, he asked me about the tramp too," replied Dr Watson. "I had no idea who the man was or what he was doing in the crypt. I doubt he had anything to do with the door. I suppose we might never know who he was. How is the job hunting going, Joseph?"

"Terrible, unfortunately," Father Sage said. "I have been knocked back at numerous interviews. Always the same story. Someone else has more experience or better skills for the role. Usually female, of course. I have heard that my references are not worth much. The bishop was rather against my views and seemed to get to the interview committees in advance."

"Sorry to hear that, Joseph," Dr Watson said. "I hope your luck changes soon. Perhaps the death of bishop heralds a better time for you."

In the corner of the room nearby, an elderly mourner stood alone, facing outward, apparently looking at the rain falling through the window. He said nothing. He just watched the group of four in the window reflection and listened.

CHAPTER 16

FRIENDS

Father Sage walked up the long and impressively wide staircase which led to the main cathedral doors. He was planning to attend mass at the cathedral, possibly for the last time. His job had been effectively outsourced, and he had been completely unsuccessful in finding a new post. He had reached a point of despair and had given up hope of finding a suitable post within the church. He had reconciled himself to relinquishing his license as a priest and instead seeking a living outside of the church.

As Father Sage walked through the cathedral lobby, he emerged into the huge and colourful circular nave. The multicoloured stained-glass panes in the beacon windows high above the nave cast the beautiful sunlight onto the walls of the side chapels surrounding the nave. As usual, the cathedral was almost deserted. There were just a handful of tourists walking around the nave with their heads turned upwards to the beautiful glass windows. The only sound was the occasional faint whisper of conversation from visitors.

As Father Sage walked around the perimeter of the nave towards the chapel where mass was scheduled, an elderly man approached him walking from the opposite direction.

"Excuse me, Father Sage. Might I have a brief word?" said the man in a quiet voice.

Joseph was slightly surprised to be approached. He did not recognise the man. He noticed a long coat, a walking stick, a suit and tie, and shiny shoes. He guessed the man's age to be between seventy and eighty years. He presumed that this must be a parishioner who had recognised him and wanted to say farewell.

"Yes, of course. I am planning to attend mass in the next half hour, but I can spare a few minutes. How can I help you?" responded Joseph.

"Let us sit down and chat," the elderly man said and indicated with his hand towards the small side chapel of reconciliation. "I only need a few minutes, Father."

Both men sat on one of the small seats in the side chapel. This was a discreet location which afforded some privacy for their conversation. The votive candles flickered, casting a moving light on the walls.

"Father Sage, let me introduce myself. My name is Brian Dowd. I represent a group of people who take a keen interest in freedom, truth, and justice. I have been asked to approach you about an opportunity." Mr Dowd paused to let this sink in.

"I see," said Joseph. *In fact, I don't really see at all*, he thought to himself.

"It has come to our attention that you are leaving your current post within the church in the near future and that you are having some difficulty finding another post," Mr Dowd continued.

"Well, yes. This is correct, Mr Dowd," replied Joseph. "Just who do you represent again?"

"The people I represent guard their privacy closely," said Mr Dowd. "We are not part of the church as such, although we have many friends in the church. We take a wider view of society, but we are sometimes able to offer assistance to people like you in situations like yours. We are a charitable organisation."

This explanation seemed to provide information without much clarity.

"I am not sure what sort of help you are suggesting," responded Joseph.

"We are in a position to give you some assistance towards finding a new post within the church, where you can continue your excellent work," suggested Mr Dowd. "We feel that it would be unfortunate if you were forced to leave the church and if you were prevented from contributing to the spiritual and moral debate in our wonderful country."

Father Sage was both puzzled and intrigued by this turn of events. *Who is this man? Who are these people he represents? This seems too good to be true. What is the catch here?* he thought. Father Sage was not familiar with good luck. He had become accustomed to being criticised—indeed, vilified—even from within the church, for being honest, sticking to his Christian principles, and thinking clearly. After years of uninterrupted setbacks, he was well attuned to failure and rejection. An offer like the one from Mr Dowd seemed a little too good to be true.

"Well, I am certainly very grateful for your offer, Mr Dowd. I would be very happy to accept any help you can offer, of course. However, I doubt that there is much you can do you help me. You see, there are some very senior people in the church who seem determined to exclude me. My flavour of churchmanship is simply out of tune with the current fashion within our church. Belief in a living Christian God is no longer in fashion. I doubt that there is anything that will change minds of those in power," said Father Sage. He immediately thought that he may have said too much. After all, he really had no idea who this man was. Criticising the church hierarchy was a mistake in the wrong circumstances. Loyalty, discretion, and obedience were valued very highly in the higher echelons of the church.

"Let me reassure you, Father Sage," replied Mr Dowd with a smile. "The people I represent know the full details of your situation. We are very sympathetic to your views on traditional Christian teaching. We are particularly keen to promote free speech, freedom of conscience, and honest debate. Indeed, we believe that many of our fundamental rights, such as freedom of speech and freedom of conscience, stem from Judeo-Christian morality. We have some influence at the very highest level. Please let me give you my business card. There is a telephone number on the card. Please consider our offer of help and ring this number. Quote my name—Brian Dowd. My personal assistant will arrange a meeting and an interview for you. I am certain that there is a situation which will be absolutely ideal for you."

Mr Dowd passed a card to Father Sage. Father Sage read the telephone number. The title on the card read Franklin Freedom Foundation.

"What are you asking in return for this help?" asked Father Sage. *Here comes the catch*, he thought.

"We ask nothing in return," said Mr Dowd. "We offer this help in the hope that you continue with your excellent work and in the expectation that you will be offered more suitable opportunities in future to advance the causes of freedom, truth, and justice, which we value greatly."

"Well, thank you, Mr Dowd. I will certainly consider your offer. I am most grateful to you and your organisation," replied Father Sage.

"Father Sage, it has been a delight meeting you," said Mr Dowd. "It is unlikely that we will meet again. I strongly recommend that you call the number on my card. May I wish the very best of luck for the future."

Mr Dowd stood and offered a hand to shake. He was clearly ending the discussion. Father Sage stood and shook the offered hand, unsure what more he should say. Mr Dowd inclined his head slightly, turned, and walked out of the chapel towards the main entrance to the cathedral.

Father Sage was left standing in silence, dumbfounded and astonished. He could not believe what had just happened. *Did that really just happen? Have I really just been offered a career opportunity by a total stranger?* he asked himself. He looked at the statue of Christ on the cross which stood in the centre of the nave, next to the white marble altar. *There is something I am missing in this matter,* he thought.

Father Sage was very sceptical about the encounter with Mr Dowd. He tried to do a little research on the Franklin Freedom Foundation but was unable to trace the organisation. He asked some colleagues, and none of them had heard of Mr Dowd or his employers. After a couple of days, Father Sage did eventually ring the number on Mr Dowd's card, in desperation more than with any expectation of success.

A lady answered his call and, after confirming Father Sage's identity, offered him an interview the following week at a central location in London. At the interview, it turned out that a post in Westminster had just become vacant, and they were looking for a priest with exactly the type of traditional views that Father Sage represented. Amazingly, a reference from Bishop Gibot was not necessary. Within a month, Father Sage was in post in London. Gift horses, mouths, and not looking were in the forefront of Father Sage's thoughts at this time.

Being a man of faith, Father Sage was accustomed to the idea of the mystery of divine providence. However, he was not familiar with much good luck in his own life. His career in the police force had been challenging. His career in the church had so far been a struggle in a different way. Recent events had caused him to question his faith often. He might not have been as surprised at this positive turn of events as a more sceptical soul. Nevertheless, it did occur to Father Sage to ponder why his good fortune had taken quite so long to arrive.

Father Sage never heard from Mr Dowd again, nor from the Franklin Freedom Foundation.

CHAPTER 17

JUSTICE

There should be a constructive accommodation with
some aspects of Muslim Law. It seems inevitable that
elements of Islamic law will be incorporated into
British law.

—*Archbishop of Canterbury,* February 2008

The General Communications Headquarters
(GCHQ) is the nerve centre for all state intelligence collection in the United Kingdom. The mission of the thousands of staff at GCHQ is to keep
the people of the United Kingdom safe by spying
on them and spying on others. Staff at GCHQ use
technology and teamwork with other intelligence
agencies to identify, analyse, and disrupt threats to
British citizens. Without close cooperation with MI5,
MI6, British police, the British military, and foreign

intelligence agencies, it would be impossible to keep the British population safe from terrorists.

Counterterrorism activities are a priority for the men and women employed at GCHQ. Covert surveillance using a range of methods is an important asset in the fight against terrorists. There are limits to the surveillance undertaken defined in British laws. There are also social and moral pressures which from time to time restrict the decisions of security agencies. There are times when security agencies must be utterly ruthless to defeat utterly ruthless terrorists. At other times, a more nuanced and sensitive approach is chosen to balance the rights of citizens to privacy and confidentiality against the obligation to protect from terrorists. This is a difficult balance for security service to retain the consent of those whom they protect.

In 1690, a thoughtful English philosopher and physician named John Locke wrote an influential small book about the nature of government, *The Second Treatise of Government*. In his book Mr Locke outlined the principle that men are free, equal, and independent in the natural state and that no man can be governed without his consent as a fundamental principle. Mr Locke felt that the only valid reason that men give up some of their freedom—and the only reason they consent to being governed by someone else—is to obtain increased security for themselves and their families.

The staff at GCHQ are fully aware of the need to undertake their secret security work while retaining the consent of the population of Great Britain. This explains why they—and the more conventional policing authorities—are sometimes reticent to step across the prevailing politically correct boundaries of any particular period. As an example, this explains why the security and police services accepted restrictions on stopping and searching people who were objectively more likely to be endangering the security of the ordinary citizen in the early part of the twenty-first century.

Mavis Beattie was a midlevel intelligence officer at GCHQ in England working on Middle East internet traffic more than three hundred years after John Locke was born. She picked up a pattern of emails, texts, and calls bouncing between Iran, Iraq, and Afghanistan which appeared interesting. She talked to her line manager, Arthur Denniston, and they agreed that she should call a local officer in the antiterrorist prevention team in northern England to discuss the matter.

Sergeant Mohammed Amin took the call on his mobile.

"Hello, Amin here," Sergeant Amin spoke into his mobile.

"Hello, Sergeant Amin. Mavis Beattie here from the GCHQ Middle East section. I am calling about some chatter we have picked up in the Iran area which seems to indicate activity in northern England of a curious nature. The internet traffic is ambiguous, but my guess is that one of the cells we are monitoring might be planning one or more events in Manchester or nearby in the next month or two. Could I send you the relevant intel to scrutinise and investigate?" asked Ms Beattie.

"Yes, of course. Please send it over. I will check it out and let you know," confirmed Sergeant Amin.

Ten minutes later, Sergeant Amin had the raw data on the screen in front of him at his desk in the highly secure section of police HQ dedicated to antiterrorism operations. He read carefully through the various conversations and coded messages. He agreed this was suggestive that at least one of the active terrorist cells in northern England was planning something worrying in a city in the region in the near future. This was not surprising. At any one time, his team alone had five to ten similar groups under close scrutiny. The intelligence and security community had been foiling one terrorist attack each week on average in Great Britain for several decades. The question was how to respond to Ms Beattie. Acting too early or too overtly risked losing the big players organising the terrorist plots. Acting too late risked disaster self-evidently.

Sergeant Amin reflected that the GCHQ team was quite keen to see action in this type of situation. He had to handle this quite delicately to avoid unwanted consequences.

"Hello, Ms Beattie," Sergeant Amin called back to GCHQ. "I agree with you that this traffic is worrying. I have spoken to my team, and we are upgrading our surveillance on the two groups who are most likely to be involved. We will keep you informed."

"Very good. Thanks, Sergeant Amin. We will let you know if there is any more substantive information," replied Ms Beattie.

Sergeant Amin moved the files he had received from Ms Beattie to an archive folder and marked these as inactive. He closed down his laptop and opened his filing cabinet where he kept his stock of burner phones and new SIM cards. He took one of each out, left his office, and walked down past the tourists and riverside restaurants to a quiet area which he knew to be outside of CCTV range.

He leant against the railings on the waterfront and waited for a few minutes to take the opportunity to use his vaping e-cigarette. He glanced on either side just to check if anyone was taking any interest in him. He did not notice anything significant along the riverbank. Just a couple of Chinese tourists messing around trying to attach a love lock onto the riverside railings.

He sat on a bench looking over the river and inserted the SIM card in the unused mobile phone. The phone lit up, and he entered a destination number for a text. He entered the following text message: "First choice of restaurant is difficult. Too busy. Suggest ditch first choice and try out the second-choice restaurant. Same time and place." He punched the send button, then removed the SIM card and battery from the phone. After ten minutes observing the tourists walking past him, he sauntered back towards police HQ. He dropped the phone, SIM card, and battery in three separate refuse bins on the walk back to his office.

The text sent by Sergeant Amin was picked up by Mavis Beattie almost immediately. She was waiting and watching, as was her job of course. She was not able to identify the exact location for the device sending the text, but she was able to confirm the city from which it was sent and the message. She was also able to confirm the timing and the destination number, which was the most interesting part. Her intercept system recognised the destination number immediately, and this confirmed something that she had suspected and wanted to confirm for some months. She knew that action was now necessary due to this development and walked over to talk to Mr Denniston again. They quickly agreed on the best course of action. This time, Mr Denniston took over and made several calls to the Manchester office in northern England. Mr Denniston also called the home office to arrange a meeting with the home secretary.

Several minutes after Sergeant Amin sent his text, Adila Barzin was sitting in her bedroom in northern England watching a film about racism in the United States. She was very entertained by the balanced perspective of the directors of the film. Racism by militant black activists in the 1970s was balanced carefully by white racists in the Ku Klux Klan. One of the Klan members tried to blow up two ladies from the black group but only managed to blow himself up by accident. *American irony at its best,* thought Ms Barzin. The script and acting were superb. The script was laced with the casual and convincingly unintentional bigotry and prejudice which was commonplace in the 1980s in the United States. *The Americans make so much effort to appear balanced that they have no clear opinions on anything,* she concluded. *This is so different from my part of the world, and of course we have God on our side. This game is really stacked in our favour,* she thought. *It is all too easy, really. How can we lose against these no-hopers? They are always trying to be so balanced and fair—they weaken themselves to the point of despair.*

Her husband, Mohammed Barzin, knocked on her door and poked his head in.

"We have had instructions to make a slight change. We are going to use the alternative restaurant as discussed last week. We need to make the necessary cooking arrangements immediately," he said.

Adila rose from her chair, put her coat on, and grabbed her backpack. Her husband also put on his coat, and they made their way to their car, a top-of-the-range Range Rover. Their sponsors had provided lavish funding for every comfort for their stay in Great Britain in gratitude for their services. They drove to a small garage on the outskirts of the city and opened the garage door. Inside the garage, there were four plastic drums and several boxes of electronic equipment, which had been waiting for them for this eventuality. They loaded the drums and boxes into the back of the Range Rover, then closed and locked the garage and drove back to their home. They parked the Range Rover in their driveway. They were certain that the vehicle registration plate would have registered on tens of CCTV cameras around the city. They knew that they must be under surveillance by British secret services, and they were content that they had shown just enough to achieve their purpose.

The following morning just before 4:00 a.m., a team of twenty officers in two vans from the Manchester Prevent team drove to the Barzin home in northern England. They parked on opposite sides of the property. They set up infrared detection equipment within their vans and confirmed that there were only two people in the property, both apparently sleeping upstairs. At exactly 5:00 a.m., the two teams of ten men broke into the property from the front and back simultaneously. They arrested and cuffed Mr and Mrs Barzin before either of them even stood up. The Barzins were driven to the secure antiterror section at police headquarters in Manchester for interviews. The forensic team moved in immediately and took the contents of the garage away for analysis. Neighbours were surprised to wake up to a major forensic crime scene next door.

Simultaneously with the raid on the Barzin home, at 5:00 a.m. precisely, a smaller team of three heavily armed antiterrorism officers opened the front door to Sergeant Amin's house in the suburbs of the city. They opened the door silently with the key they already had. Sergeant Amin was only slightly surprised to be woken by three colleagues from another city reading him his rights and handcuffing him. Sergeant Amin's career as an antiterrorism officer had come to an abrupt halt. He had been expecting something like this at some point ever since he joined the national antiterrorist Prevent team.

Several days later at GCHQ, a case conference was convened by Mr Denniston, with Mavis Beattie and officers from the Manchester office. After a brief presentation of the facts, Mr Denniston summarised the situation so far.

"It seems that the message traffic we intercepted from the Middle East from Sergeant Amin and from the Barzins related to an attempt to plant a rather large explosive device in the cathedral, probably in the next week or two. Preparations were at an advanced stage. Ms Beattie and her team deserve the credit for solid work there." Mr Dennison nodded towards Ms Beattie, who beamed appropriately.

"The explosives we found were certainly sufficient to destroy the cathedral and kill anyone inside at the time. Sergeant Amin and Barzins have been relatively cooperative since their arrest. A guilty plea from all three is likely, according to the interrogating officers. We have been worried about Amin for some time and were monitoring his communications.

"Amin has dual nationality, and the home secretary has ordered the removal of his British citizenship. He will probably be deported to Iraq after trial and conviction to serve his sentence in jail there. The Barzins are both from Afghanistan and travelling under false papers. They will likely remain in custody indefinitely since deportation to Afghanistan is not viable. They are being surprisingly helpful with details of their plan. The home secretary is very pleased and sends her thanks to all involved. Great work, team."

The trial of both of the Barzins took place in the Queen Elizabeth Crown Court, within a few miles of the planned terror attack, with reporting restrictions put in place by the trial judge. The reporting restrictions prevented any publication of the identity of the accused or any specific details of their alleged crimes while court proceedings were ongoing. The judge put these restrictions on free speech in place in order to ensure that both defendants received a fair trial and to ensure that any jury would be unaffected by partisan media reporting.

Gerard Harrison, a local journalist, waited outside the court on the first morning of the trial. He had spoken to his employer's legal advisers and clarified the precise details of the court order relating to the trial. He had been advised that he could video the defendants arriving at the trial outside of the courtroom and stream this live to his website but that he must not mention the names of the defendants or the exact location of the alleged crimes or the trial. He intended to publicise as much about the trial as was legal in order to raise public awareness to warn his fellow citizens about the risks they faced.

Mr Harrison was writing and publishing about the effect of high levels of immigration because he felt this threatened the British culture which he loved. He had previously brushed against the British legal system during his work and had suffered some criticism and penalties as a result. This did not deter him. He did not feel that he had consented to the huge cultural changes which he had witnessed in his hometown, and he felt a duty to shout loudly about these. His motives were remarkably similar to the good people working at GCHQ. They all wanted to maintain the security of the citizens of Great Britain.

The two prison vans arrived close the court, and the two prisoners were escorted towards the court. As they walked up the wide stairs past the statue of Queen Victoria, Mr Harrison started videoing their approach and spoke a quiet commentary into his mobile phone. He was careful not to give names or exact details of the alleged crimes. He did outline an alleged terrorist bombing and confirmed the city where the alleged crimes were planned.

As he was videoing, Judge Godfrey Mason QC was watching from the large window in his rooms in the Queen Elizabeth II Crown Court. He knew about Mr Harrison and did not agree with his political views.

He saw Mr Harrison videoing the approach of the defendants and immediately summoned the senior security officer on duty that day.

Sergeant Leonard King arrived a few minutes later at the judge's rooms.

"Sergeant, I want you to arrest that man." The judge pointed out of his window at Mr Harrison, who was still standing on the stairs approaching the court and talking into his mobile phone. "I believe that he has disobeyed the court order in relation to my case today. Please arrest him, detain him, and confiscate his mobile telephone. Bring the telephone to me here in my rooms."

Sergeant King looked from the window, nodded, and said, "Yes, Your Honour. At once, Your Honour."

Mr Harrison was arrested by four burly police officers. He asked in vain for the reason for his arrest. He videoed their approach and the conversation with the policemen until the point that his mobile phone was confiscated. His video was streamed online and went viral amongst the tens of thousands of supporters who sympathised with his views about balanced immigration. He was not aggressive to the policemen, and they were very polite but firm with him.

Judge Mason briefly reviewed the online video material, which was by then openly available on the internet, from his desk workstation. He was satisfied that the legal restrictions had been breached. He ordered the court clerk to list an immediate hearing relating to contempt of court. An hour later he was facing Mr Harrison in court.

The QC representing Mr Harrison at short notice had advised him to plead guilty to contempt of court. He had advised Mr Harrison that the judge was likely to give a suspended sentence or possibly a community service order and that they would easily overturn this on appeal. He was not familiar with all of the context of Mr Harrison's past legal entanglements. After all, he had only been given an hour to prepare for this hearing.

"How does your client plead to the charge?" asked the clerk to the defense QC.

"Guilty, Your Honour," said the lawyer in open court.

Judge Mason nodded with satisfaction. He turned to Mr Harrison in the dock.

"Mr Harrison, you can remain seated. On this day, the eighth of May of this year, in the course of ongoing proceedings for allegations of terrorist offences faced by two defendants at this court, that trial still in fact being in progress, you attended, together with another, and carried out some filming. That filming was firstly on the approach to the court and then on the steps at the front of this court building, although of course, I readily accept there was no filming or attempt to film inside a courtroom.

"The only person who was filmed was effectively yourself. You provided a spoken commentary with your filming. Both of those to-camera pieces were immediately published on the internet, by live-streaming, in various forms as I understand it, but under the heading 'Gerard Harrison in England exposing Muslim terrorists.' Your intention in being at this court and in carrying out the actions that you did was, on your own account, to inform and warn the general public about this trial. It had come to my attention, via the good offices of my security staff, that you were present and what you were doing, and as a consequence I gave directions in order to ensure that both the jury, and in due course the defendants, were escorted from court by different routes in order to avoid there being any kind of confrontation or interference. That was not a decision that I took lightly because, of course, diverting the jury from anything other than their usual route may have given rise to questions in their mind about what was going on and why. This could prevent the defendants from receiving a fair trial.

"When you were outside the court, you were within the precincts of the court. When you were on the steps leading into the court building, you were effectively and self-evidently in the court building. There are notices all over the court building and precinct making it clear that filming or the taking of photographs is an offence and may be a contempt of court. You were told very clearly by security staff at this court that you were to stop filming and that if you continued filming then you would be potentially committing an offence and may be held in contempt of court. You continued filming despite these instructions and warnings.

"I am told that it was not your intention to frustrate the court process. In fact, you claim that it was the opposite of that. I accept your statement about your intention. These were deliberate actions on your part. They were deliberate actions intending to take photographs of the trial location. They were actions which you continued to take, despite having been told that you should not do so. I find, as a clear logical inference, that your intention on coming into the court building was to seek out the defendants, whom you referred to in the way in which we have all seen and heard. You made it abundantly clear—indeed, it is abundantly clear—that your mission and purpose was to identify the trial and publish this information. By filming and publishing in this way, even though you had been told not to, these matters were then published to a very wide viewing audience. You referred to the defendants by their religion and referred to them as 'Muslim terrorists.'

"This contempt hearing is not about free speech. This is not about the freedom of the press. It is not about legitimate journalism. This is not about political correctness. This is not about whether one political viewpoint is right or another. It is not about making judgements about any religion or culture. It is about justice, and it is about ensuring that a trial can be carried out justly and fairly. It is about ensuring that a jury are not in any way inhibited from carrying out their important function. It is about defendants being innocent until proven guilty. It is not about people prejudging a situation and going 'round to that court and publishing material, whether in print or online, referring to defendants as 'Muslim terrorists.' This is pejorative language which prejudges the case, and it is language and reporting that could have had the effect of substantially derailing this trial.

"As I have already indicated, because of what I knew was going on, I had to take preventative action in order to make sure that the integrity of this trial was preserved, that justice was preserved, and that the trial could continue to completion without people being intimidated into reaching conclusions about it or into being affected by irresponsible and inaccurate reporting. I may now face applications from legal advocates to abandon this trial. If something of the nature of that which you put out on social media had been put into the mainstream press, it is even more likely that I would have been faced such applications from the legal advocates concerned—either to give specific instructions to the jury to protect the defendants or, worse, to abandon the trial altogether. This is the kind of effect that actions such as yours can and do have. That is why you have been dealt with in the way in which you have and why I am dealing with this case with the seriousness and speed which you see.

"I find that your actions constitute the commission of an offence under Section 41 of the Criminal Justice Act 1925. You have apologised for what you have done. I have to say, I find it really rather difficult to accept your apology at face value, given your background. I have been told that you have previously been given different advice at a different court about what you could or could not do in terms of filming and broadcasting. This is no concern of this court in relation to this trial. Notwithstanding anything you may have been told elsewhere, at this court, you were told in clear and no uncertain terms—on more than one occasion—that you could not film.

"In my judgment, an apology is not sufficient. Neither do I feel in this case that a financial penalty is sufficient in itself. It seems to me that this does need to be met with a custodial sentence and a fine. The only question in my mind is whether you might be placed in potential danger were I to send you into custody. Would you stand up, please?

"I take a very dim view indeed of your conduct which was in the face of repeated warnings that you should not do that which you did do. I accept the dangers that you might face were you to be sent into immediate custody. However, you could be put into protective custody. The sentence, therefore, that I pass upon you, taking into account all of those matters that have been placed before me, is one of two years' imprisonment and a fine of two hundred thousand pounds."

There were audible gasps from various people in the court. Such a sentence, delivered at such speed and in secrecy, was astonishing in the British legal system. Mr Harrison stood with his mouth open in astonishment and looked at his barrister. The barrister was equally dumfounded and simply stared back. Mr Harrison's colleagues and friends were effectively prevented from being in court due to the secrecy and rapid speed of the proceedings. The judge also continued the imposed reporting restrictions on the terrorism trial and on Mr Harrison's hearing for the duration of the terrorist proceedings. By the time any of Mr Harrison's friends and family heard about this matter, he was safely tucked up in prison.

The secrecy surrounding this entire matter had the paradoxical effect of heightening the interest of the wider media in this case. As a result, all of the mainstream news outlets on TV and in newspapers ran headline stories speculating about the fate of Mr Harrison and the nature and danger of secret trials. The terrorist trial was even more widely reported than Mr Harrison had intended despite—or possibly because of—the best efforts of the judge to suppress free speech and freedom of the press.

The trial judge was correct to be concerned about defense advocates asking for the terrorist offences to be dismissed on the grounds that his clients were unable to receive a fair trial due to adverse reporting. After legal arguments lasting several days, the case against the Barzins was dismissed on the grounds that they could not receive a fair trial, and the Barzins were released. None of the court proceedings resulting in abandonment of the trial were published due to the restrictions placed by the courts, thus saving the blushes of the home secretary.

Mr Harrison was placed in protective custody in prison. His new lawyers assured him that he would certainly win an appeal against his conviction. His supporters started a crowdfunding attempt to raise funds to pay his substantial financial fine and to pay for his defense costs.

Three months after he commenced his custodial sentence, he was found dead in the shower area within the prison. He was hanging by his neck from the showerhead by a belt. He had apparently used someone else's belt to hang himself. The source of the belt was never discovered. At a subsequent coroner's inquest, a verdict of suicide was recorded. Reporting restrictions continued to restrict the public awareness of these events even after his death.

With legal aid from the British taxpayer, Mr and Mrs Barzin, who were Afghan citizens, applied for compensation for wrongful arrest and detention. Their application was successful, and they were awarded in excess of one million pounds' compensation. Reporting restrictions prevented the general British public from being informed about this rather expensive and embarrassing matter. Thus the good reputation of the home secretary was preserved at the British taxpayers' expense.

Some days after the release of the Barzins, in a large compound in Pakistan, near the capital Islamabad, several men were meeting to discuss a project they had been planning for some years. The hot, dusty compound was surrounded by a high wall which was at least twelve feet high at the lowest point. There were no aerials or satellite dishes on the buildings in the compound. All of the men had to surrender their mobile communication devices some miles from the compound, and they were escorted to the meeting by a small group of armed security guards.

The obvious leader of the group was dressed entirely in black with a black turban. He spoke gently with authority, and the others listened silently when he spoke.

"Thank you for coming to this meeting my friends," he started. "As you all know we were successful in purchasing some very special fuel from those kafir in Russia who have a taste for material wealth. This fuel has now been shipped to the destinations where we plan our celebrations. Our brothers and sisters in Britain have done well. The plans we made for all eventualities appear to have worked there. The flexibility which we built into our plans has proved necessary. The temporary fuss has settled after our brother and sister offered themselves as a diversion. The primary objective there remains on target. Within a short time, we will see another strike against the satanic forces in the West. Our plans in the Great Satan are also coming to maturity nicely. Thank you for your support brothers. God is great."

"God is great," his colleagues repeated, echoing his religious call.

On the same day as the meeting in Pakistan, another meeting was taking place in England. Archbishop Graham Brown, the archbishop of Canterbury, had planned to speak publicly about his plans to bring all Christian faiths, Judaism, and Islam closer together for many months. He was presented with the perfect opportunity when he was invited to be a member of the BBC television panel on the programme *Question Time.*

The question seemed innocuous enough. A Scottish lady from the audience asked how the panel planned to reduce the level of threat from religious terrorists in Great Britain. The answers of several panellists were the usual bland speech ignoring the question, accusing their political opponent of racism, and condemning whatever was in their political opponents' policy. The archbishop's answer was different.

"In my view, there is a relatively straightforward solution to this issue. It may not be easily achievable, but it is straightforward," offered the archbishop initially. "For several years, it has become clear to me that my branch of the Christian communion is losing the battle for minds and hearts. We are being outpaced by our competitors who have a better offer for members. As a result, we are closing churches at an escalating pace. It is embarrassing for me to admit that other faiths are often opening these churches which they then fill with the faithful. I speak mainly, of course, of the Islamic faith which is growing at a rapid pace both here and abroad.

"My response to this is to build bridges with my fellow faith leaders. To this end, I have been in discussions with colleagues in other branches of Christianity as well as leaders of the Jewish community and Islamic leaders in Britain. I believe that we are close to reaching a historic agreement between the leaders of all Abrahamic faith systems in this country. In the near future, I believe that we will agree to the joint use of the building for worship in Britain and to mutual recognition of Islamic sharia law, Christian canon law, and Jewish Halakha law. I believe this will be the culmination of more than two thousand years of dialogue. We will in effect be able to set up a new holy empire or caliphate, starting in Britain and hopefully then spreading worldwide. In my view, this is the best route to peace."

The audience in the BBC studio reacted furiously to this announcement. The word "caliphate" seemed to be the most offensive part of the speech.

The popular press the following day were hardly less angry than the studio audience. There were accusations that Archbishop Brown was a closet Muslim. Muslims objected vocally and violently in street protests to the idea that they would be forced to worship in the same building as Jews. Jewish leaders objected to the thought of sharing places of worship with Muslims and Christians. Christian leaders, including the freshly appointed Bishop Joseph Sage, were outspoken in their refusal to accept this merger of religions. There were numerous death treats aimed at the archbishop from Muslims, Jews, and Christians. Security measures to protect the archbishop had to be augmented considerably. Within days several potentially fatal packages were intercepted in the post by the security officers.

Soon after the fateful television program, the archbishop offered his resignation to the king. Officially he announced his retirement. In truth, he was resigning for his own safety. He agreed to stay in post until a suitable successor could be found.

The discussions on joint buildings of worship and mutual recognition of religious laws did not prosper after Archbishop Brown left office.

CHAPTER 18

PERSISTENCE

Muslim majority Tunisia bans the burqa in public buildings after bombings.
—*Associated Press,* 2019

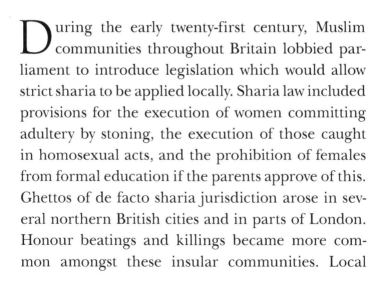

During the early twenty-first century, Muslim communities throughout Britain lobbied parliament to introduce legislation which would allow strict sharia to be applied locally. Sharia law included provisions for the execution of women committing adultery by stoning, the execution of those caught in homosexual acts, and the prohibition of females from formal education if the parents approve of this. Ghettos of de facto sharia jurisdiction arose in several northern British cities and in parts of London. Honour beatings and killings became more common amongst these insular communities. Local

law enforcement professionals found little cooperation from the general public in such communities.
Legal authorities and law enforcement professionals
were hampered in their duties by "hate crime" laws
which persecuted anyone expressing concern about
the rapid pace of cultural segregation. The accusa-
tion of Islamophobia was used to stifle any criticism
of religious ideology. A powerful lobby pushed for
Islamophobia to be classified as a form of racism,
which would have made criticism of Islam illegal.
Blasphemy laws were creeping back into British
culture.

In Detective Inspector Malcolm Everton's family, there was a tradition of public service in the
British police force and armed services. Kenneth
Everton, Malcolm's father, had served in the British
Army during the Second World War. In this struggle against Nazi oppression, Sergeant Ken Everton
was part of the Special Boat Service, an elite team
within the Royal Navy. Ken was parachuted into
northern France many times for missions to prepare
for Operation Overlord, the invasion of Normandy
in 1944. Ken blew up bridges, railway lines, and
ammunition depots and assassinated numerous

high-ranking German officers. He operated alone most of the time. After each mission, he swam out to a prearranged rendezvous with a British submarine and escaped back to England. The risks for Ken were considerable. The mortality rate for officers with his role was in excess of 40 percent per mission. However, Ken was good at his job and survived. He took part in the missions which were covered dramatically in the film *A Bridge Too Far*. Ken did not receive any official recognition for his bravery and skills during the war due to the secret nature of his role.

After the war, Ken joined the police force in a northern England cathedral city. One feature of Ken's personality was a fierce adherence to ethical standards and a refusal to compromise standards. He thought for himself and did not allow anyone to dictate his views to him. One evening in the 1950s, Ken was on duty and was called to the scene of a burglary at a shop selling alcohol and cigarettes. He found several junior police constables at the scene of the burglary. They were busy loading boxes of cigarettes and whisky into their police patrol car. Ken was the senior officer at the scene. He singlehandedly arrested all of the police constables, drove them to the local police cells, and locked them up for the night. He ensured that they were all fired from the police force and prosecuted for their actions. The discipline of police officers under his supervision was perfect from that time forward.

Detective Inspector Malcolm Everton had inherited the streak of fierce determination and free-thinking that characterised his father's personality. Malcolm did not like being told what to think or say.

Some days after his interview with Superintendent Richards, Inspector Everton was reviewing the file on Bishop Gibot's death. He was considering the pros and cons of pursuing the various lines of enquiry that still existed. He was particularly thinking carefully about Ms Adila Barzin. It was clearly very satisfactory that the security services had been alerted to Mohammed Amin's double role. The seizure of the explosives at the Barzins' home had officially been a triumph for the security and police services. However, Inspector Everton had a slight concern about the conclusion of this matter.

Until the day before their arrest, the Barzins had maintained a high level of secrecy about their plans. The CCTV footage confirmed that the Barzins had driven to a storage lockup the day before their arrest and loaded their car with high explosives. They had then parked their car—full of explosives—in the driveway of their suburban home in full view of all of their neighbours. They must have known that their car would have been registered on CCTV systems. Yet they made no attempt to use alternative vehicles, store the explosives at an alternative site, and insulate themselves from the explosive plot.

Why did they park the car full of explosives overnight at their home? Why not just leave the explosives in storage until it was time to move them to the intended target? What was the real target? During police interviews, the Barzins and Mr Amin had both maintained that they were waiting for instructions on where to place the explosives. They claimed that they moved the explosives the day before their arrest because they were tipped off that the storage facility had been compromised. The collapse of their trial had halted any further interrogation of the Barzins. The security services seemed satisfied with the outcome and were not inclined to look further into the events leading up to the arrests.

But Inspector Everton had a bad feeling. He was very uncomfortable with the fact that Superintendent Richards had virtually instructed him to back off the investigation into Ms Barzin. Why was it so important to the terrorists that they had to corrupt the police investigation and thereby risk exposing their double agent in the Prevent team? The whole matter felt like a much larger issue than a relatively simple terrorist bomb which would have killed a few dozens of people at most.

Inspector Everton decided to look at the matter from the other end. Rather than trying to deduce what the terrorists were planning and projecting what their ultimate aim was from their known actions so far, he decided to look for any potential terrorist targets—big targets—in the region in the near future and work back from them to a potential terrorist plot. He searched for significant events and celebrations of Western democracy which had prominent national figures attending in the near future.

He found three possible celebrations which might attract terrorist attention. There was an anniversary of the bombing of St Paul's Cathedral in the last World War. However, this was in London, and the Barzins and Mr Amin were located in northern England. A large celebration for the global circumnavigation by Sir Francis Drake was planned, but this was largely centred on the south coast of England at naval bases. Finally there was a service of commemoration planned at the Metropolitan Cathedral of Christ the King to commemorate the first-ever visit of a British monarch to the Vatican. This was an ecumenical celebration, and many senior religious figures were slated to attend, as was the king of England and the prince of Wales. This ceremony was only two days away. The crowds were not expected to be huge. It was more of interest to those very involved in religious issues and watchers of the Royal Family, rather than a truly international cause.

Inspector Everton scratched his head and wondered. Would a terrorist want to disrupt the celebration of reconciliation between the Vatican and the British monarchy, which had technically persisted since Henry VIII had turned his back on Catholicism? *Perhaps I should ring GCHQ?* thought the inspector. He'd tried several times to contact Mavis Beattie at GCHQ without success. Ms Beattie was tied up dealing with an attempt to sabotage British shipping in Gibraltar by Iranian terrorist cells. In the end he slept on his concerns and tried again to ring Ms Beattie the following morning with more success.

"Hello, Ms Beattie," said Inspector Everton on the telephone to GCHQ. "I am very sorry to bother you. I just have some loose ends to tie up about the Barzin affair up here in the north."

"No problem, Inspector. How can I help?" responded Ms Beattie.

"Well, I am a little puzzled by some of the events leading up to the arrest of the Barzin couple. They seemed to maintain a high level of secrecy about their plans until the day before their arrest. Then they seemed to abandon all common sense and security by driving their own car to the storage lock-up, loading enough explosive in their car to blow up their own home, then parking their car full of explosives in the driveway of their home overnight in full view of all of their neighbours.

"They must have known that their car would have been registered on CCTV systems. Yet they made no attempt to use alternative vehicles or store the explosives at an alternative site. They made no attempt to insulate themselves from the explosive plot. It seems almost as if they suddenly wanted us all to be attracted to them. During police and security service interviews, they claimed they were waiting for instructions on where to place the explosives because of a tip-off that the storage facility had been compromised. But surely they would have used extra precautions to conceal themselves and the explosives if such a tip-off had been received?" asked Inspector Everton.

Ms Beattie considered for a few seconds and then replied, "Yes, I can see that this is not very neat and tidy, Inspector. However, we did identify and foil a serious terrorist plot, and recover a relatively large amount of high explosive. Terrorists sometimes panic and behave foolishly when they fear they are discovered. Also, the collapse of their trial and the disastrous outcome of their appeal have severely limited our ability to make any further legal approaches to the Barzins. The courts would shred us, and the media would have a field day if we pressed this matter further with the Barzins without cast-iron evidence of guilt. They would play the race and religious discrimination card. I can make some enquiries from my seniors and the home office if you would like me to."

"Yes, thank you, Ms Beattie. Just to put my mind at rest, I would value further instruction and guidance," replied Inspector Everton.

Several hours later, Inspector Everton's phone rang. By this time it was late afternoon on the day before the celebration at the Cathedral of Christ the King.

"Hello, Inspector," said Ms Beattie. "The response I have received from my line management and the home office is very negative. I have been told in no uncertain terms to drop this matter. The home secretary does not want any risk of adverse publicity from the Barzin trial fiasco. The government wish to avoid any risk of allegations of Islamophobia. "

"Right. Thanks so much, Ms Beattie. I will take this on board," replied Inspector Everton.

The following morning, the day of the cathedral celebration, almost as soon as the inspector arrived in office, there was a tap on Inspector Everton's door, and Superintendent Richards entered without invitation. She closed the door and stood facing Inspector Everton. *She must have been waiting for me to arrive this morning. I am popular,* thought the inspector.

"Malcolm, sorry to intrude unannounced like this," said the superintendent. "I just had the most extraordinary telephone call. It was from the home secretary himself. Not a common occurrence, as you might imagine. He is up in arms about the Barzin trial mess. He tells me that you are still chewing this one over, and he wants us to shut up and close the case. I was rather embarrassed to have to tell him that I thought it was all over and done with."

"Ah, yes. I was going to contact you, ma'am. I just wanted to check with GCHQ first, and I think they alerted the home office before I even had a chance to see you."

"So the Gibot case is closed and you are not hounding the Barzins," suggested the superintendent. This sounded more like a statement than a question.

"Err, yes—just the final paperwork to write up. That's all, ma'am," said the inspector.

Pressure from the home office and Superintendent Richards did not succeed in putting Inspector Everton off the scent. He did not take well to being told to shut up. When Superintendent Richards had retreated to her top-floor office, Inspector Everton rose from his desk and walked out of the police HQ. *I am missing something obvious in this case. I need to see things with fresh eyes*, he thought to himself. *Perhaps I might get some inspiration from a reexamination of the house the Barzins were arrested in.*

He drove to the Barzins' old house on the outskirts of the city. *There must be some clue here in the Barzins' house to indicate what was really going on*, he thought.

He spent several hours going through the Barzin house with a fine-tooth comb. There was not a single indication of any other plan that he could find. He reflected on his findings—or lack of findings. Inspector Everton had been a keen fan of Sherlock Holmes stories in his childhood. He recalled the famous fictional detective telling Dr Watson, who had been to Afghanistan with the British military, to eliminate all factors which cannot be true, and whatever is left must be the truth, however unlikely it seems. So since there was no indication of any other plans for the Barzins, then the Barzins had no other terrorist plans. *But…what if the Barzins were a decoy? What if we were meant to capture the Barzins and find their explosives to put us off the scent of another, bigger plot?* Inspector Everton's mind was racing. *Perhaps I am looking in the wrong place,* he thought. *Perhaps another device has been in position all along in the cathedral.* There were fewer than three hours before the start of the large gathering of VIPs in the cathedral. How could he prevent the celebration from taking place? He had no evidence. There was no way he could persuade the king, the prince of Wales, the archbishops, and the rest of them to cancel the event—just on the basis that he had a hunch—with only a couple of hours' notice.

He drove at a high speed through the suburbs towards the city centre.

CHAPTER 19

NEVER GIVE UP

British Home Office declares that Christianity is not a religion of peace.
—*Daily Express,* 2019

MI5 confirms that the number of terrorist cases related to radical Islamic terrorists dwarfs the number linked to far-right groups.
—*Guardian,* 2019

Old, white, liberal, British broadcaster objects to "so many white people in one place" at a Brexit rally in London.
—*Channel 4 News,* United Kingdom, 2019

Danish government bans foster parent in retaliation for publication of videos of radical Islamic terrorists killing Danish citizens.
—*DR Network,* Denmark, 2019

By the time DI Malcolm Everton arrived at the city centre, there were already road blocks in place preventing any road traffic from entering an exclusion zone surrounding the cathedral for a mile in all directions. Malcolm had to abandon his car and walk or run the rest of the distance to the cathedral. Duty police constables stopped him twice on the way because he was running. He was in plain clothes, of course. It was only by showing them his police warrant card that he could continue. He arrived at the cathedral to find a large crowd surrounding the cathedral, waiting outside to catch a glimpse of the king, the prince of Wales, and any other celebrities who might emerge.

His first task was to get inside the cathedral. There were uniformed police officers posted at all entrances as well as burly security officers in dark suits watching the crowd with professional, detached calmness. He also noticed several snipers lurking on rooftops surrounding the cathedral. *I had better watch my step, or I might end up being picked off by a twitchy sniper,* he thought ruefully.

There is no way to get through the crowd to the main entrance. Perhaps I should call Superintendent Richards before I dive in on my own, he thought as he gazed over the heads of the crowd up the steps leading to the cathedral's main entrance. His heart was racing, his hands were shaking, and his palms were sweating. He struggled to dial the number for the superintendent. She was not answering her phone.

He ran around the side of the cathedral from where he could see the underground car park entrance. This led directly underneath the cathedral. There were officers in uniform and plain clothes guarding the entrance. He approached the entrance with his warrant card held out in front of him. A burly security officer with a bulging suit held up his hand and stepped forwards to prevent him from entering.

Malcolm started speaking. "I am terribly sorry, Officer. I am DI Everton from the city police force. I have reason to believe that there may be some form of terrorist plot taking place here today. I need to get inside the cathedral to look for any signs. Could you let me into the car park and I will take it from there, please?"

The security officer was taken aback. He took Malcolm's warrant card and studied it closely.

"Just one moment please, Inspector," he said politely. He turned away while raising his concealed radio to his mouth.

After several minutes, the security officer turned back to Malcolm. "I understand that Superintendent

Clarissa Richards will be ringing you on your cell phone, sir," he said.

At that moment DI Everton's mobile phone started ringing.

Malcolm answered the call. "Superintendent Richards speaking. Is this DI Everton?" asked the caller.

"Yes. DI Everton here, ma'am. I am very sorry you have been bothered. I have reason to suspect that another explosive device has been planted somewhere in the cathedral area. I am trying to get into the cathedral to find any evidence. It would be very helpful if you could persuade the security officers here to let me into the cathedral."

"And precisely what is this new evidence that you have stumbled across at such a late stage, DI Everton?" asked the superintendent.

"I called at the Barzins' house earlier and couldn't find anything. It occurred to me that the only logical explanation for the fact that the Barzins made it so easy for us to catch them red-handed was because they wanted to be caught. The only reason I can think of for this is that they wanted to distract us from something else and put us off guard. Something even bigger and more dangerous. It is a huge coincidence that this cathedral celebration today includes the king, the prince of Wales, and numerous other dignitaries, just after we were all distracted by our apparent triumph over the Barzins which has lowered our guard—"

"So let me get this right," interrupted Superintendent Richards. "You have a hunch that there is a second bomb in the cathedral because the bomb we found previously was too small for your liking, and we were too successful in foiling their plot. Is that your great theory, DI Everton?"

Malcolm swallowed hard. *When put like this, the whole theory does sound somewhat tenuous,* he thought.

"Well, yes, ma'am, I suppose my suspicions are based on the relative ease with which we prevented the first attempt," replied DI Everton.

"Right. Listen very carefully to me, DI Everton!" shouted Superintendent Richards into her phone. "If you go anywhere near the inside of that cathedral, I will have you dismissed from the force quicker than you can blink. I have every liberal human rights lawyer in the county bleating in my ear ten times a day about misogyny and Islamophobia. It has taken over a decade of hard work for us to recover the reputation of the police in this country from being institutionally racist. And you are pursuing an investigation against a religious minority—probably also a racial minority group—and almost certainly a female on the basis of your hunch. Get away from that cathedral, and I want you in my office at nine a.m. tomorrow when we will consider your career options. Have I made myself clear, DI Everton?"

Malcolm paused before replying. The security officer had been standing and listening only a few feet away. He gave Malcolm a supportive and silent shrug in recognition of an irresistible order from a senior officer.

"Yes, ma'am. I will see you in the morning," replied Malcolm.

Malcolm ended the call and replaced his mobile phone in his pocket. He looked at the security guard but was at a loss for words.

"Listen, mate," the security guard said in a low voice after a few seconds. "I can see you are very worried, but there is nothing I can do to help you officially. I suggest you go 'round to the other side of the cathedral. The crowds are much thinner over there. There might be a bit of space where you can think more clearly. Don't do anything rash. Do what you know is right."

Malcolm considered this advice briefly.

"Thank you. I am Malcolm Everton, by the way," he replied. "I'll do as you suggest."

"My name is David—David Johnston. Good luck, Malcolm."

The two men shook hands and parted on good terms. Malcolm walked slowly around the cathedral towards the opposite side to the main entrance. The crowds gradually thinned out, as did the level of security, as he walked. After a few minutes, he had reached the far side of the cathedral. He walked down a flight of stairs leading from the cathedral concourse to the street level. There were several seats conveniently situated for the public in this area, and Malcolm sat on one of them to clear his mind.

He sat staring at the cathedral for several minutes. *Am I right to be this concerned*, he thought, *or am I just imagining the danger?*

As he sat thinking, he realised that there was a locked double door in front of his seat. The double door was clearly an entrance to the crypt under the cathedral. It may have been an entrance for suppliers at one time, but it appeared to have been unused for some period. It was locked with a small rusty padlock only. Malcolm's heart started pounding again. He knew that he had to get into the cathedral if this was at all possible. His doubts disappeared instantly. Any concerns he may have had for his own career evaporated. His only thought was to save the people in the cathedral, including the king, the prince of Wales, and all the other innocent celebrants.

He checked the roofs of surrounding buildings. He could not see any snipers directly from his seat. The door was even more shielded by the overlooking cathedral concourse.

He stood and walked as calmly as he could to the door. He slipped his car key into the small rusty padlock and twisted. The padlock disintegrated easily. He opened the double doors and slipped inside the crypt.

The crypt of the cathedral was deserted and quiet. Malcolm could see no signs of security or cathedral officials. He walked past the exhibits of church gold, silver, and embroidered vestments in their shiny glass cases. The tomb with the rolling door came into view on his right side. Malcolm reflected on the events on the day that Bishop Gibot died. *This is all part of the same ongoing cultural problem*, he thought to himself.

Malcolm reached the entrance to the administration offices, which were also underneath the cathedral. This time there was no lock on the door. He passed silently through and into the administration corridor.

What am I looking for? he thought.

As he stepped down the corridor, he heard some voices which appeared to be coming from one of the offices. He carefully opened the door of an adjoining office and stepped inside. It was dark and empty. He left the door open just a tiny crack to let some light in from the corridor and listened at the wall. There were definitely several people in conversation in the next office.

A sound from the corridor caught his attention, and he stepped quietly to the door to peer out into the corridor.

Two figures dressed in the burqa and niqab emerged from the adjoining office—one short and one at least a foot taller. They were talking quietly in Arabic. One voice was female, but the other was definitely male. *Call me old fashioned and prejudiced if you like, but that is definitely a man under that veil,* thought Malcolm. The two figures walked away from Malcolm and passed through the exit from the administration corridor.

Malcolm opened his door and quickly moved to the next office. He tried the door, and it opened. He stepped inside the office and closed the door.

The room was fully lit. A bank of computer screens filled one wall. Some complex machinery and electronics filled the middle of the room. At the heart of this machinery stood a large and shiny, rectangular metallic box that was about the size of a coffin.

Malcolm was uncertain what to do. *This could be the device I was looking for,* he thought. He had no idea how to defuse any device like this. He checked his mobile phone. No signal. *Of course,* he thought ruefully.

He bent over the metallic box, looking for any sign of a control mechanism. He noticed some writing on some of the attachments bolted to the main box. *That looks like Cyrillic, Russian writing,* he thought. *This is not at all good. I need some urgent help from the bomb squad.*

Something hit him hard on the right shoulder. He knew there was pain in his shoulder, but time seemed to slow down and the pain seemed to belong to someone else.

He tried to turn towards the door, but four hands were holding him tight. Two hands were enclosing his waist, and two arms were wrapped around his neck. He struggled to move at all and fell forwards onto the machinery in the centre of the room. His forehead struck a protruding steel bolt and started bleeding profusely into his eyes. He tried to call out, but the arms around his neck prevented any sound from emerging.

Seconds passed, and his vision started to become white.

Suddenly the two sets of arms crushing him seemed to release their grip. He gasped for air and found he could move and breathe again.

A hand reached around and lifted him away from the machinery. He looked up into the face of David Johnston, the security guard. Mr Johnston was holding a large wrench. The two figures dressed in burqas were lying on the floor, clearly unconscious. A pool of blood was collecting under the head of one of them.

"Well, you are a really determined chap," said David with a smile. "I thought you might find a way into the cathedral. I followed you through the crypt entrance after I found the broken lock. The way that Richards bird talked to you was completely out of order. If I had been your boss, I would have made a visit to these offices myself to ensure the public were safe. Looking at all this, I am glad I did."

Malcolm sat on the floor and breathed deeply.

"Thank you" was all that Malcolm could say for a couple of minutes.

Both David and Malcolm looked around at the machinery and the computer screens in the office.

"How in heaven's name are we going to disable this complex bit of equipment?" asked Malcolm, pushing himself up from the floor.

"I have no idea. But first I have to try to start an orderly evacuation of the building, and get hold of the bomb squad," replied David.

The security officer raised his wrist-mounted two-way radio to his mouth. "This is David Johnston. I am in the cathedral admin section with DI Everton from the local force. We have stumbled onto what appears to be a large explosive device. I recommend immediate evacuation of the entire cathedral complex. Repeat—immediate evacuation. Also I need to get hold of the bomb squad immediately. Can you patch me through to them please?"

Suddenly Malcolm remembered the Russian writing. He groped for his mobile phone and tried to steady his hands to take a photographs of the Cyrillic writing and the overall device. He emailed this to his colleague at police headquarters with a short message to get the pictures to the bomb squad immediately and to get urgent advice on defusing the device.

"David, I have sent pictures of this writing and the device to police headquarters," said Malcolm breathlessly. "They will send the pictures over to the bomb squad. Can you ask your contact to get the bomb chaps to contact us directly and perhaps we can do something useful under their direction."

"Good thinking Malcolm," replied David. He spoke briefly into his radio, asking for urgent contact with the bomb experts.

It was 2:58 p.m. The British monarch and the heir to the throne were in the cathedral with hundreds of other dignitaries. The policeman and the security officer turned to the explosive device and wondered how they were going to disable the detonator.

CHAPTER 20

CABINET ROOM A

The British government committee that meets during national emergencies is called COBRA. This stands for Cabinet Office Meeting Room A, which is where the committee meets.

The prime minister ran his hands through his blond hair. It stood up like a bleached, disordered, spiky toilet brush as usual. He turned to the home secretary. The committee, which he chaired, had invited various security and scientific experts to give a presentation and update them.

The prime minister spoke to bring the meeting to order. "Let's get going, then. Thank you everyone for coming today. We have Professor Sheila Gordon from Cambridge, who is a radiation expert, and Arthur Denniston and Mavis Beattie from GCHQ, who are experts on the security background. Professor Gordon, please, could you briefly summarise for the benefit of the cabinet members?"

Professor Gordon stood and started her PowerPoint slides with a remote device.

"Thank you, Prime Minister. Just over three months ago, at three p.m. on the second of July, while a packed cathedral ceremony was in full swing, a nuclear device detonated beneath the Cathedral of Christ the King."

The professor brought up an aerial photograph of the crater which had replace the cathedral on the screen.

"The blast from the nuclear explosion yielded the equivalent of one hundred thousand tons of high explosive. The fireball radius was five hundred metres. Within this radius, the temperature was hot enough to vaporise all life forms and all buildings. Everyone in the cathedral died instantly. The cathedral itself disappeared into the blast crater. The thermal radiation radius stretched three miles from the explosion in every direction. All humans within three miles of the cathedral were killed within hours of the blast due to severe burns. Radioactive fallout travelled several hundred miles in all directions over several days as the winds moved around, and it was detectable on continental Europe within twenty-four hours. In the past three months since the explosion, more than half a million people have lost their lives.

Radioactive fallout has now been detected in the United States, Japan, and Australia.

"In the immediate aftermath of the explosion, on scientific advice, the government has declared an exclusion zone with a diameter of twenty miles from the blast centre for the foreseeable future, while clean-up plans are being developed and implemented. This exclusion zone includes several neighbouring towns and cities which have been evacuated. Almost two million British citizens are being permanently relocated throughout the British Isles. It is hoped that this evacuation and resettlement will be complete within six months. A huge programme of home building has commenced, with the armed services helping civilian contractors. The public has been informed that it will be many decades before the city will become safe for habitation again. In fact, the scientific committee has advised senior politicians that the likely timescale for the radiation levels to normalise is probably more like twenty thousand years. This fact has not been given to the general public yet in the interest of maintaining public order.

"Thank you, Professor Gordon," interrupted the prime minister. "Perhaps it would be helpful for Ms Beattie to update us about the security background now."

Mavis Beattie stood and took the PowerPoint control from Professor Gordon. She brought up a picture of Detective Inspector Malcolm Everton in his police uniform onto the screen.

"The nuclear device was planted by a group of religious extremists who had infiltrated the cathedral staff. They were employed as religious liaison officers and had full access to the cathedral complex, which had very light security protection. We have been able to confirm that those killed included Detective Inspector Malcolm Everton from the city police force and Detective Sergeant David Johnston from the Royal Protection Command Service. At the moment of the explosion, these two police officers were in the cathedral trying to defuse the detonator. Sergeant Johnston had just asked for a full evacuation of the cathedral site, and was being connected to the bomb squad, when the blast occurred. It appears that Inspector Everton had attempted to persuade his superior officers to stop the ceremony and evacuate the cathedral earlier in the afternoon of the explosion. His request was turned down, and he was ordered to leave the area of the cathedral by a superior officer. The perpetrators of this atrocity had fooled the police and security services by preparing a decoy device, which we discovered a short time before the nuclear explosion. This misled us into thinking that we had successfully foiled the attempt."

Ms Beattie sat, and the prime minister spoke again.

"Thank you, Ms Beattie. As we all know, also killed instantly were the reigning monarch, his heir, the outgoing archbishop of Canterbury, two other archbishops, dozens of senior religious leaders from many different faiths, and at least four hundred community leaders from many different organisations in northern England. These people were all vaporised in an instant. These two brave policemen died as patriots trying to save their king and their fellow countrymen from a violent death. They were doing their best to save everyone in the face of severe pressure to do nothing on the grounds of political correctness. Malcolm Everton's senior colleagues in the police force did not listen to his concerns because they were scared of offending a religious minority group and activist feminist groups. I understand that the previous home secretary was also somewhat complicit in ignoring DI Everton's warnings. The avoidance of causing offense had become more important than the avoidance of violent terrorism. Keeping the general public safe had been relegated to a second priority. This is an unacceptable situation, and it must be corrected in my view. This nuclear explosion has changed the nature of geopolitics and our attitude towards religious extremism for a generation or more throughout the world."

The prime minister turned to the new home secretary. "Nigel, what do you feel about this catalogue of misery and failure of intelligence?"

"Well, I agree with you, Prime Minister," replied the home secretary. "I think this has been a terrorist atrocity waiting to happen. Ever since we opened our borders in the last century and introduced politically correct laws which tied the hands of the police and the security services, the terrorists have been holding all the cards. In particular, the hate speech laws have had a chilling effect on the very necessary public debate on important issues like mass immigration, deportation, and immigration checks. Since the speech by Enoch Powell in the 1960s, free debate has been stifled in our country, and our political leaders have been reluctant to speak out. We are wasting a huge amount of police time investigating and prosecuting comedians for making jokes about the Nazis instead of pursuing those who hate our culture and want to destroy us.

"The British police and security services came very close to foiling this latest terrorist plot. If the two unusual deaths related to the fire in the Irish Centre had been investigated with more vigour, it is likely that the cause of two deaths by radiation poisoning would have been confirmed at an earlier stage. Two such identical deaths of this nature might have raised the suspicions of the security services about an impending nuclear terrorist threat to a higher level. If the police enquiries into Ms Barzin had not been discouraged on the basis of political correctness and if they had they been pursued with more enthusiasm at an earlier stage, it is possible that details of the origin of the radioactivity might have been traced.

"If there had been better communication between the security services at GCHQ and the local detective, Inspector Everton, a link between Ms Barzin, radioactivity, and two unusual deaths might have been made. If the security services had been less satisfied with the conventional explosive identified in the dawn raid, they might have found evidence of an even greater threat to explore. The failure to conceal the explosive more effectively might have raise suspicions about this being a decoy. On a broader canvas and over a longer timeline, if we and other Western democracies had encouraged oppressive governments in the Middle East not to suppress free expression so ruthlessly in their countries when they achieved independence from colonial rule in the twentieth century, then their citizens might have found a more peaceful outlet for their frustrations locally and might have felt less inclined to seek sanctuary in plural secular democracies such as Great Britain.

"This might also have reduced the likelihood that those accustomed to a culture of religious obedience and intolerance would have felt impelled to lash out against our culture of individual freedom and tolerance. If our activist judiciary had been less willing to impose secrecy on terrorist trials and if the concerns of journalists like Gerard Harrison had been given more attention, then he and many others might still be alive. The British police, security services, and courts are rightly concerned to avoid allegations of racism and sexism. But they were wrong to discourage publicity just because a suspect was female and from a particular religious or cultural group. However, in defense of the police and security services, it is politicians who pass laws on free speech, hate crimes, and offensive language, and it is politicians who define the legal limits for security services. Simply to speak is to risk offending someone. To give offense and to feel offended are very different concepts. When thinking and speaking offensively are criminalised, free speech is discouraged to a dangerous extent in my view, Prime Minister.

"Many tens of thousands of souls were extinguished in a moment by the terrorist nuclear bomb planted under the Cathedral of Christ the King. Countless further thousands have been maimed or disabled for life by the blast, fires, and subsequent radioactive fallout. Our neighbours in other countries in northern Europe are also affected, of course. Crops grown and livestock reared within the nuclear fallout area will have to be destroyed for several years, which will have a devastating economic impact on the farmers of Europe.

"Most of those who planned this atrocity were safe and remote from the effects. As we now know, they also carefully prepared their messages for the international media before vaporising their victims. The bombers claimed that they represented something called The Movement for True Believers. You have all seen their message sent in text and email form to most of the world press, which read, 'We honour our God by destroying the work of the unbelievers.' They had smuggled the nuclear device into the cathedral basement by dismantling the device and concealing it in delivery vehicles and under their clothing. CCTV records which survived from outside of the city confirm that the terrorists used religious clothing such as the burqa as a method of disguise to smuggle equipment into the cathedral basement.

The presence of the religious liaison office in the cathedral administration offices aided their subterfuge since the security staff became accustomed to seeing Muslims coming and going on routine business at all times of day and night. The underground car park beneath the cathedral, which did not have adequate CCTV, also helped them transport logistics for such an enterprise. Most of the bombers were men, but they remained undetected due to the eagerness of the British establishment to respect religious dress codes irrespective of risks of terrorism.

"To summarise, Prime Minister, this is a total disaster. We need to repeal the laws against free speech and enable our security services to investigate and apprehend all those who threaten our security, whether they are female, male, black, white, Christian, or Muslim. I have received generous offers of help from all of our allies, including, of course, the United States."

"Thank you, Nigel," responded the prime minister. "That was quite a speech, with much of which I fully agree. It is reassuring that you still feel fully able to indulge in free speech. I am pleased that we have a clear idea of what our priorities are at this stage."

The prime minister then turned to the two security officers.

"Thank you, Mr Denniston, and thank you too, Ms Beattie. We value your summary of events greatly. In many ways, you did a wonderful job. You foiled one attack and successfully apprehended three terrorists. Sadly, a second and far larger attack was successful. The causes of our failure to foil the second attack are clearly multiple and span many functions of government and the security services. We will consider carefully your full report and then decide on appropriate action. Your country greatly values your service."

This was in effect a dismissal, and the two security officers left the COBRA committee room.

Once they left, the prime minister turned to the remaining members of the committee. "Whatever else we do, I agree with the home secretary that we need to repeal the laws encroaching on free speech as a matter of urgency. Protecting ourselves from nuclear bombs is far more important than protecting ourselves from offensive jokes by insensitive comedians. Nigel, please submit a new bill repealing all relevant legislation by Friday."

"Yes, Prime Minister," replied the home secretary with his well-recognised broad grin.

A year later the COBRA committee was still meeting weekly to manage the strategy for recovery from the nuclear explosion.

In a break with precedent, the president of the United States had been invited to attend one COBRA meeting during a state visit. This was a move which reflected the close cooperation between the two democracies.

The prime minister opened the meeting with a brief summary of events.

"I would like to welcome our friend, the president of the United States, warmly to our meeting today. I can confirm that following the genocide in England last year, the process of reviewing the practice of all religions is well underway. Any religions which promote violence or intolerance are now banned or restricted in Great Britain, most Western European countries, Canada, Australia, and New Zealand. We have received excellent cooperation from the leaders of all religious groups in Britain. Perhaps you might outline the steps you have taken in the United States, Mrs President." The PM turned to the president.

President Owens cleared her throat. "Thank you so much, Prime Minister, for inviting me to your meeting today. First, I must offer my thoughts and prayers for those who were injured in the explosion and the families who have lost loved ones.

"As you all now know, your nuclear device was the first of four which the terrorists intended to detonate. The American people and all people in the world owe your Detective Inspector Malcolm Everton a great debt of gratitude. His quick thinking in sending photographs of the device and the labels, just minutes before detonation, was crucial.

"After your MI6 passed the images to our CIA, we were able to trace the source of the nuclear fuel used within a matter of hours to a military base in Russia. We contacted President Mironov in Russia as soon as we knew it was of Russian origin. To her credit she was very helpful. With the help of the Russian Secret Service, the FSB, the Russians were able to locate the corrupt officials who sold the nuclear fuel to the Pakistani terrorist cell. With unprecedented cooperation from the Pakistani government, it was then relatively simple to locate the compound where the terrorist leaders were living, extract them from their hideaway near Islamabad, and induce them to cooperate. We knew the locations of the remaining three devices within 24 hours of the detonation in England. These devices were located in New York, Washington and Philadelphia. The terrorist's plan was to detonate all three bombs in the United States on our Independence Day, which would have over-whelmed our emergency services, and killed count-less millions. We were able to intercept the terrorists, before they were able to finalise their preparations. All of the devices in our cities were successfully de-fused, less than 24 hours before they were due for detonation. The assistance of President Mironov has helped to save many million American lives. We have had our differences with the Russian Federation and the Pakistani government, as you know. However, President Mironov and the Pakistanis have shown on this occasion that terrorism arising from religious ideology is a shared enemy for us all.

"In recognition of the enormous contribution that he made to the security of the United States and world peace, I will be awarding the Presidential Medal of Freedom posthumously to Malcolm Everton. It is a small token of our undying gratitude for his sacrifice.

As you know the First Amendment to our Constitution forbids us from prohibiting any reli-gion. However, instead of this, we have introduced security measures which dramatically increase our surveillance of any religious institutions and any preachers which are known or suspected of radical-ising the vulnerable or fomenting violence. The pro-cess for comprehensive vetting of immigrants to the

United States has been accepted across our political spectrum, ending decades of opposition from those who claimed the title of 'progressive.' I know that some Western countries have started a programme of wholesale compulsory demolition of mosques. This is not something we have implemented in the United States. In line with many other free democracies, on grounds of public safety, we have restricted face covering, such as the traditional dress of the burqa and niqab in public places, education, and hospitals. Schools and universities which we found were promoting religious intolerance and inhibiting free speech have had their state funding removed. We have found that this brings about a pretty rapid change of attitude and policy in these institutions. They seem to have suddenly rediscovered their original enthusiasm for the principles of free speech and tolerance again. Like you we have also empowered our police and security forces to adopt all means of keeping our citizens safe. This includes stopping and searching all suspected criminals. As a woman of colour, I am proud that we have removed the limitations on stop and search activities. Our police and security forces are once more colour blind.

"You may all know that the United States of America's founding documents include a list of natural rights which our founders believed were inalienable for all people. These rights were considered natural rights. This means that our founders did not consider that these rights were granted to us as a gift by any government or ruler, and therefore these rights could not be taken away from us by any government. With good reason, the wise men who founded our republic considered the very first in the list of these rights to be the freedom of speech in all its manifestations. These founders considered themselves British until the rupture in 1776 and derived their constitution from principles outlined in your British common law and statutes such as the Magna Carta and the British Bill of Rights, which include freedom of speech.

"You all know about our withdrawal from the United Nations. When the UN Security Council failed to condemn the nuclear atrocity in unambiguous terms, we coordinated with your great country and other allies to withdraw from what we view as a fatally flawed organisation. We are very grateful for the assistance of Great Britain and the leadership shown by your prime minister for the new coalition of plural, freedom loving, democratic countries, which we are calling the United Democracies. We have agreed with all allies to impose economic and military sanctions on military and theocratic dictatorships in the Middle East and Asia. The new United

Democracies happens to consist of almost all of the wealthiest countries in the world, of course, constituting more than eighty percent of global GDP. Our democracies together account for GPD of over $60 trillion in a world which generates $75 trillion annually. Our coalition of wealthy democracies carries immense influence due to our financial and economic power. We are no longer timid about asserting our economic power, which we believe stems from our free democratic ethos. The sanctions have already resulted in a dramatic and speedy abandonment of nuclear aspirations by several previously hawkish nuclear aspirant nations, as you all know. Our first Secretary General of the United Democracies, Canadian Professor Peter Jordan, spoke eloquently a short time ago in his inaugural speech about the importance of challenging intolerance in all forms and of the value of free speech as a foundation for democratic and peaceful government by consent. Our First Amendment has effectively been adopted as the prime human right in the founding document of the United Democracies. Thomas Jefferson, who considered himself British until 1776, of course, would be pleased as punch if he only knew about this.

"I believe that Charles Pierre Baudelaire, the nineteenth-century French poet, is credited with the statement that 'the finest trick of the devil is to persuade you that he does not exist.' Some believe that the devil takes many forms. The fact that nuclear radiation is invisible to the human eye makes it an invisible killer, and therefore very difficult to defend against. Nevertheless, we must strain all of our sinews to combat this menace, and especially to keep this material out of the hands of fundamentalist religious terrorists.

"Prime Minister and my friends, it is a paradox, but one unforeseen and accidental result of the tragic death of hundreds of thousands in England could well be said to have been a dramatic reduction in the risk of nuclear proliferation elsewhere in the world for decades, along with an explosion of freedom amongst previously oppressed countries. The best solution to religious terrorism has turned out to be more freedom for more people. Who would have thought this? Previously intransigent dictators and theocracies have become much more willing to redraft their national constitutions to inch towards plural democracy, regular free elections with secret ballots, term limits for elected leaders, freedom of expression, as well as the separation of executive, legislative, and judicial branches in government. A terrible human cost had been paid for this paradoxical result.

"I believe that your prime minister Winston Churchill once reflected on the fact that we can be counted on to do the right thing, after we have tried everything else. My friends, after a few missteps in the 20th century, I believe that together, across the free democratic world, we are now finally starting to do the right thing."

CHAPTER 21

THE KING

The cabinet finds it undesirable that face-covering clothing, including the burqa, is worn in public places, for reasons of public order, security, and protection of citizens.

—*Dutch Immigration Minister,* 2006

Austria's government will close seven radical Islamic mosques and expel dozens of foreign-funded imams. Vice Chancellor Heinz-Christian Strache remarked, "We're only just getting started." This is part of the government's campaign against radical Islamic ideology and the influence of countries like Turkey in the Austrian Islamic community.

—*Kronen Zeitung,* June 2018

British soldiers who criticise a politically correct army recruitment advertisement, which shows a

patrol stopping to allow a Muslim soldier to pray, will be punished.
　—*Mail on Sunday*, August 2018

Conservative member of Parliament faces formal investigation for comparing women wearing burqas to letterboxes.
　—*Daily Telegraph*, August 2018

Pakistan-born former bishop of Rochester calls for ban on full face veils, supported by former archbishop of Canterbury.
　—*Breitbart London*, August 2018

French President asserts that "true" Frenchmen "do not exist," supporting a globalised EU superstate.
　—*Breitbart London*, August 2018

Sweden Democrat Party leader wants Sweden to leave the European Union. No supranational body should have authority over the Swedish Parliament.
　—*Sveriges Radio*, August 2018

Women's March in London cancelled because it would be "overwhelmingly black."
　—*Eureka Northern California*, 2018

Belgium bans halal and kosher slaughter methods.
—*Daily Express*, 2018

European Union grants ten million euros of taxpayers' funds to study the Qur'an.
—*Il Giornale*, 2018

Muslim girls not allowed to eat lunch until after boys at school.
—*Daily Telegraph*, 2019

Grand Mufti of Australia confirms Muslims should never disavow verses in the Koran which incite violence.
—*SBS News*, 2019

Oxford University redesign classics courses because men achieve too much success.
—*Daily Telegraph*, 2019

Cheshire police reject outstanding candidate because he was a straight white male.
—*ITV News*, 2019

Jews are the first victims of Islamic immigration.
—*Die Welt*, 2019

Pakistan prime minister claims there is no mention of Jesus in human history, but the life of Muhammad is part of history.
—*Times of Israel*, 2018

Islamic State celebrates destruction of Notre Dame Cathedral. Say goodbye to your polytheistic temple.
—*Terrorism Research Consortium*, Paris, 2019

King George VII, the king of England, stood before the archbishop in Westminster Abbey.

"Sir, is Your Majesty willing to take the oath?" intoned the new archbishop.

"I am willing," answered the king.

The archbishop continued. "Will you solemnly promise and swear to govern the peoples of the United Kingdom of Great Britain and Northern Ireland, Canada, Australia, New Zealand, and of your possessions and the other territories to any of them belonging or pertaining, according to their respective laws and customs?"

"I solemnly promise so to do," answered the king.

"Will you, to the utmost of your power, maintain the laws of the United Kingdom of Great

Britain and Northern Ireland, Canada, Australia, and New Zealand, as well as of your possessions and the other territories? Will you, to the utmost of your power, maintain and preserve inviolably in the United Kingdom the freedom of speech, freedom of the press, the right of the people peaceably to assemble, the right of the people to establish and practice peaceable religions, and the right of the people to petition government for redress of grievance, as by law established in England? And will you preserve unto the people of England all such rights and privileges as by law do or shall appertain to them or any of them?"

"All this I promise to do," the king responded.

The oath sworn by King George VII differed significantly from all previous coronation oaths. Gone were references to the unique protections for the Church of England and the unique protections for the "rights and privileges of the bishops and clergy of England." This marked the end of just over five centuries of special privilege accorded to the Anglican Church which began with Henry VIII exercising his royal power in search of a male heir in 1527. For the first time in English history, a monarch had sworn to protect "peaceable religions" but not all religions. Those religions which promulgated violence and hatred were on notice that their time was coming to an end. Freedom of speech and freedom of the press were now accorded priority over establishment of a state religion. This was a significant constitutional development in Great Britain.

The king arose from his chair as the sword of state was carried before him. He walked to the altar and made his solemn oath in the sight of all the people, laying his right hand on the Holy Gospel in the great Bible, which was offered to him by the archbishop as he knelt on the altar steps.

"The things which I have here before promised, I will perform and keep. So help me God," the king announced.

King George kissed the book and signed the oath. His coronation was effectively complete.

Archbishop Joseph Sage rose in front of the king and turned to bless the congregation.

Archbishop Sage's promotion to the highest office in the Anglican Church had startled him in its rapidity after the nuclear disaster. As a recently promoted bishop in London, his public warnings about the dangers of the toleration of religious bigotry had received widespread support from the British public and increasing support in the British media. His predecessor, Archbishop Graham Brown, had been vaporised in the nuclear explosion after being hounded by the press following his appearance on the popular television question programme shortly before the nuclear atrocity. Archbishop Brown had proposed a merging of mainstream Christian, Jewish, and Islamic faith systems into a global religious caliphate or empire. The use of the word "caliphate" had been an excruciating error on his part.

There had been a strident outcry from most religious commentators. Notable support for Archbishop Brown came from some religious leaders in the Middle East but not from Israel. It had been Archbishop Brown's misfortune to make his proposal public only weeks before the nuclear religious protest which killed more British people than the Second World War. He had then planned to retire to seclusion, with an armed guard, on the advice of the British police because they could not guarantee his safety if he continued in office. The search for his successor was underway when the nuclear atrocity occurred. He had the bad luck to be in post still when the celebration was scheduled at the cathedral. This effectively accelerated his retirement on a permanent basis.

After the nuclear atrocity, Archbishop Joseph Sage moved quickly to rescind previous pronouncements endorsing sharia law. Archbishop Sage reasserted traditional Christian religious teaching on the exceptional nature of Christian belief in the literal resurrection of Christ, the sanctity of marriage as a relationship between a man and a woman, and the opposition of the Anglican Church to the ideology of gender fluidity or denial of biological gender. Archbishop Sage also supported the disestablishment of his own church—the Anglican church—and the protection of all peaceable religions under human rights legislation in order to protect the independence and freedom of all peaceful organised religions. In the fraught atmosphere after the nuclear atrocity, there were few who chose to oppose these measures.

Today, Archbishop Sage was crowning King George VII because his father and grandfather had been killed in the cathedral conflagration. The double assassination was indeed the first part of the plan of the religious terrorists who had timed their barbarity to remove the reining British monarch and the first in line of succession. A young King George VII was enthroned a year after losing his grandfather and his father.

While the ceremony progressed in Westminster Abbey, the centre of what was left of the cathedral city in northern England where the nuclear explosion occurred was almost deserted. A few military drones hovered overhead, unobserved by most of the population and media. They were monitoring the radiation levels and keeping an eye on the safety perimeter set up by the government on a permanent basis.

During the coronation ceremony in London, hundreds of miles north of London, close to the centre of the exclusion zone, where the cathedral crypt used to be, a relatively flat area of rubble and concrete now existed. All of the buildings in this area had been reduced to rubble and dust or melted by the explosion. Across this barren landscape, a lone figure was strolling slowly, looking carefully at signs of the blast. The twisted and blackened steel and masonry on which he looked was within a few hundred metres of the epicentre of the nuclear explosion.

The figure was dressed in what appeared to be a long coat, and a hat hid his face. It appeared to be an elderly man. He supported himself with a walking stick as he walked with a limp across the rubble. On this day of the enthronement of a young British king, he gazed on a scene of warlike destruction, which had once been one of the largest cities in England. The presence of this figure had been noticed by the drones which the security services used to monitor the exclusion zone. The security staff were used to deranged and confused people straying into the danger zone. It was impossible to police the entire perimeter all of the time.

"There is another crazy in the hot zone," the duty drone officer based at the security surveillance centre in Yorkshire spoke to his colleague. They both looked at the screen and shook their heads. Radiation levels were too high within the inner exclusion zone to permit survival. Sadly, this man was doomed to die a painful death from radiation exposure. There was nothing they could do.

CHAPTER 22

REFLECTIONS

Ten thousand Islamic radicals demand global blasphemy laws and rally in Pakistan against a "Draw Mohammed" contest in the Netherlands.
—*The Washington Post*, August 2018

Turkish President attacked Austria's impending closure of mosques and expulsion of imams, saying, "These measures are leading the world towards a war between the cross and the crescent."
—*AFP News Agency*, June 2018

Hate preacher released from prison after less than three years despite being dangerous. The preacher says, "When sharia law is implemented, the queen will be expected like all women in Britain to be covered from head to toe, only revealing her face and hands. By 2050, Britain will be a majority-Muslim country. It will be the end of freedom of democracy

and submission to God. We don't believe in democracy. As soon as they have authority, Muslims should implement sharia. This is what we're trying to teach people. Next time when your child is at school and the teacher says, 'What do you want when you grow up? What is your ambition?' they should say, 'To dominate the whole world by Islam, including Britain—that is my ambition.'"
—*Daily Telegraph*, September 2018

Far-left Islamic activist calls for dehumanisation of Israelis.
—*The Algemeiner*, September 2018

German Supreme Court rules that the ban on child marriage under sharia law is unconstitutional.
—*Breitbart News*, 2018

Canadian Islamic cleric announces that wishing fellow Canadians "Merry Christmas" is worse than murder.
—*Middle East Research Institute*, 2018

Belgian MPs vote to ban the burqa.
—*Daily Telegraph*, England, April 2010

French MPs vote in favour of banning burqa.
—*Daily Telegraph*, England, July 2010

Australian court orders Muslim witness to testify without burqa. Judge of the Perth District Court said that it was "inappropriate" for the woman…to have her face covered while testifying.
—*Daily Telegraph*, England, April 2010

Austria burqa ban: Government warns Muslim women to show faces in public or be fined.
—*The Independent*, England, September 2017

It was a beautiful autumn day on the southern coast of England.

Dr Neil Watson walked slowly up the narrow street in the centre of Selchester and wandered into his favourite secondhand bookshop, Reid's Secondhand Books, to peruse the delights on offer. He found an autobiography of his most reviled prime minister. The Cheshire Cat grin shone out at him from the book cover. At £1.50 secondhand, the hardback was a bargain, and Dr Watson rapidly concluded the purchase. He was particularly content that the money went to the shopkeeper, Mr Reid, and not to the prime minister who had done so much to damage the country. He walked uphill with his book wrapped in a brown paper bag to hide his guilty pleasure.

He arrived at the Selchester Cathedral refectory ten minutes early. He was meeting Archbishop Sage for lunch. They had started meeting for lunch at the Selchester Cathedral refectory after Dr Watson's enforced move following the nuclear terrorist atrocity. Dr Watson had only survived the explosion because he and his wife had arranged to meet Bishop Sage in Kent on the day that the bomb exploded. Father Sage was already in his new post in London and had been promoted to the post of bishop. With incredible luck, they had arranged a pilgrimage to Down House, the home of Charles Darwin, on the same day as the explosion.

Dr Watson had not been able to return to the north due to the nuclear exclusion zone, of course. He had moved to Selchester near the south coast of England and retired almost completely from medical practice. The two men had resumed their previous habit of weekly lunch meetings, which had started when Dr Watson was a junior doctor and Joseph Sage was a student of theology. Their conversations would have still seemed tedious and repetitive to any observer. They discussed matters of religion and politics as usual. Although these two subjects had potential for significant intolerance and dispute be-tween them, this did not seem to affect their friendly dialogue. The fact that they rarely reached any con-clusion—and the fact that they seemed to cover the same ground repeatedly—did not seem to inhibit them from talking endlessly about these subjects.

Dr Watson sat in the window of the refectory with his pot of tea and sandwiches. He looked out onto the steps leading up to the Norman cathedral. Not for the first time, he thought to himself that it was impressive how those with supernatural beliefs were inspired to build such beautiful and impressive buildings in which to worship. A small group of Asian tourists was collected at the foot of the steps. Judging by their serious attitude towards taking photographs of themselves with the cathedral in the background, they too were impressed with the building.

Dr Watson checked his mobile phone for a text from Archbishop Sage. As was usual, the archbish-op was a little late for the lunch meeting. A text an-nounced that the archbishop would be arriving in a further ten minutes.

Twenty-five minutes later, Archbishop Joseph Sage entered the refectory and waved to Dr Watson. He was dressed in civilian clothes, cotton trousers, and a fleece made of recycled plastic bottles. Dr Watson recognised the fleece and thought again that this was a little too eco-sensitive and political-ly correct for his taste. The only sign of the arch-bishop's archbishopric was the small, silver, pectoral cross hanging around his neck from a green and gold cord. Once he had purchased a baked potato and pot of tea, he joined Dr Watson sitting in the refectory window. He arranged his cutlery and tried to pour a cup of tea. As usual most of the tea ended up in his saucer or on his tray.

"Why can't we design tea pots that transfer tea into the cup rather than spraying it around the ta-ble?" asked the archbishop rhetorically.

"Well, it can't possibly be your fault that most of the tea missed the cup, can it?" suggested Dr Watson helpfully. "What a fabulous day," he continued, changing the subject.

"Yes, indeed. I often think that autumn in England is my favourite season," the archbishop said in agreement.

"So how is retirement treating you at the present, Neil?" asked the archbishop.

"Well, I am certainly enjoying the extra free time. As is often the case, although I have officially retired, I still do the occasional medical clinic, but I keep this to one day per week or less. The free time has allowed me to finish writing my novel, which has been gestating and slumbering for years, as you know. You are aware that it is not particularly politically correct of necessity considering the subject matter. With the old antifree speech—so-called antihate speech—laws, I am not sure it would have even been legal to publish it if I had finished it. Now that free speech has been reinstated by our great new prime minister, I have been able to publish it. However, I am writing it for myself, really, and for you to enjoy, of course. In truth, I enjoy the writing more than the thought of publishing. Retirement also lets me visit more art galleries than was the case when I was in full-time medical practice. And you? How is the church treating you?"

Several decades previously, Dr Watson and the then-Father Sage had agreed that they would both try to write a novel within five years. They both had strong beliefs which they wanted to explore and disseminate in a novel. They had tried to encourage each other in this, but their aspirational timescale had slipped time and time again. Ten years had become twenty, and still they were both still trying to write.

"Busy, busy, busy as usual," replied the archbishop. "I find the work very rewarding, though. My novel is not progressing at all sadly. Not enough hours in the day. As you say, since the new laws on religious freedom and freedom of expression were passed, we no longer have to worry about expressing opinions about repressive behaviour from other organised religions and from militant atheists. It feels as if everyone can breathe more freely in the current legal climate. Inevitably, we have to tolerate some abusive and offensive attacks about our Christian beliefs. However, we are used to this, and freedom of speech means freedom for our opponents too, of course. We have thick skin and can take quite a lot of criticism."

The two friends ate quietly for several minutes, each thinking back over the momentous events since their student days many decades previously.

"My thoughts often stray back to Leonard Gibot. It occurs to me that he was only a product of his time. I wonder how much blame can realistically be attached to Leonard for all of the intolerant and discriminatory policies he followed and for the catastrophic events which unfolded," suggested the archbishop.

"I am not so sure, Joseph," replied Dr Watson. "Leonard Gibot was a complete ass. He was an alcoholic without any principles. He was a dishonest and manipulative racist. His only aim was to progress his own career and increase his own personal power. He never cared about your church or your religion, really, in my view. He was a blatant racist against those with dark skin in his youth. He then hid his prejudice against dark skin and homosexuality when these became inconvenient. Instead he adopted views which were equally intolerant of white skin and heterosexuality because this was then preferred by the progressive lefties in power.

"You have to admire his flexibility, but ultimately he was a complete hypocrite, devoid of principle. He actively fostered intolerance, and in doing so, he encouraged the intolerant and their violent actions. The one redeeming feature of his life was that he saved your life. By dismissing you, he ensured that you would be moving to London and that you would no longer be incinerated by the nuclear terrorist outrage. Indirectly he therefore ensured your promotion to your current position. Indirectly, I suppose, he also saved my life since you invited me to visit Darwin's house on the precise day of the nuclear explosion. Since Gibot did not do these things on purpose and they were just happy accidents, I cannot give him any personal credit."

"You are right, of course," agreed Archbishop Sage. "But we all have personal ambitions, and I still feel that Leonard Gibot had some redeeming features which were only visible on very close inspection. He did seem to be working to bring those of different beliefs together. Do you feel that we made any serious mistakes? Were either of us without fault in how we behaved towards the bishop? Should we have done more to oppose his misguided projects?"

Dr Watson thought carefully for a few minutes before replying. "I don't want to say too much about this, of course," replied Dr Watson. "Were we without any fault? I guess not. Is anyone ever without any fault in any complex situation? We are mere mortals. Not everything we did was perfect. We all had choices between several undesirable options. Charles Lambert and George Peterson are dead today because of the terrible choices of religious terrorists. They are not dead because of our decisions. Charles, George, you, and I took action in relation to Gibot's medication and the door to the tomb that day in an attempt to stop him in his crazy crusade which was destroying the church. He was even rumoured to be next in line for the archbishop's post. We chose the least bad of the options available to us. Bishop Gibot and others in senior church positions were dismantling the entire foundation of Christian life and indeed undermining ancient British values of freedom. All four of us opposed almost everything Bishop Gibot was doing in our different ways. Life is never perfect in these decisions.

"Did we do the right thing in the end? Yes, on balance, I think we did. George, Charles, you, and I all made choices which were for the greater good to benefit the maximum number of people, even if we sinned according to the Christian God. If we had done nothing, matters could have become even worse, and Bishop Gibot could have caused incalculable harm to our society. Was our chosen path without risk? No, of course not. Were there disadvantages to what we did? Yes, there were many. However, not acting was also a dangerous course. We could not have known about the terrorist actions which were about to occur. Did our actions contribute to the terrorist bombing? Of course not. The evidence from the popular press suggests that the terrorists were on an unstoppable course to catastrophe, irrespective of our actions.

"Did our actions contribute eventually to a better country with more tolerant and liberal laws which allow greater freedom of expression and freedom of worship? It is hard to know. In a small way, I think we might have helped. Your appointment to a senior post is one positive outcome that none of us could have anticipated. The bombing, of course, had a much larger effect on national and international policy. Would I do the same again if we were in the same situation? Yes, definitely."

"Overall, I agree with you, Neil, of course. My God commands me not to breach his Ten Commandments. I accept my own sinfulness, and I repent my sins. I ask for forgiveness from my God, and I hope he offers this to me. I can do nothing else. You should try this too. You may find it rather effective," suggested the archbishop.

"We are in agreement with Your Grace," joked Dr Watson. "Apart from the fact that I do not have your supernatural beliefs, I fully agree that we should recognise and repent our mistakes and seek forgiveness for these where possible. I don't accept all of your Ten Commandments, but I have ethical principles which are similar to—and indeed are derived from—some of the Christian rules. I too accept my part in this entire matter. Only you and I really know the truth, and I suspect this will die with us."

After a further hour of rather circular and fruitless but very enjoyable debate, the two old friends left the refectory and wandered slowly up the steps to the cathedral doors. Once inside, they walked around the almost empty and ancient nave. They paid the fee and walked down the stone staircase to the crypt under the nave. As they approached a tomb where Saint Richard of Selchester was buried, they both stopped and stared past the stone entrance to the tomb. Two old men queueing outside a tomb of a man long dead, waiting for their turn to enter.

EPILOGUE

MI5 confirms that Radical Islamic Terrorism remains the most acute threat to the British people.
—*London Evening Standard,* 2019

Preferred terms are now "climate emergency" rather than "climate change" and "global heating" rather than "global warming." There is no need to have a "denier" to balance debate.
—*Guardian Newspaper,* England, 2019

New Islamophobia definition is a "bullies charter" for Muslims to censor criticism of Islam.
—Former head of British Equalities Commission, 2019

Silencing unpopular opinions is not a violation of free speech. Some debates should be shut down.
—*Guardian Newspaper,* England, 2019

British police pay £2,500 for wrongful arrest after arresting a Christian preacher in London and confiscating his Bible for preaching and saying he did not agree with Islam.
—*The Mail on Sunday*, England, 2019

⇥ ⇤

What is the best way to settle a debate—censorship or more debate?

The answer to this question might have seemed straightforward in 1514 to Nikolaus Copernicus or later to Galileo Galilei and to Charles Darwin. And yet Copernicus was too scared to publish his ideas before he died, Galileo was imprisoned and forced to declare something he knew to be untrue, and Darwin delayed publishing his ideas for decades. It seems that this principle of open debate was not at all self-evident to the Pope and cardinals who had political power and censorship powers in the sixteenth century. Or perhaps the principle was obvious to them but they were corrupted by power and the desire to preserve that power.

By the twenty-first century, censorship of civilised debate was surely a thing of the past, or so many thought at the opening of the new millennium. Surely this was so, after centuries of religious wars and many violent revolutions in Europe to establish natural rights, democracy, and freedoms for the common man.

Fate offers us one or two examples of contemporaneous issues which illustrate why we might still question how secure free speech is in the twenty-first century.

Firstly, there is climate change. Debates and publication of data and theories about climate change seemed to be conducted in a spirit of openness and transparency during the twentieth century for the most part. There did not seem to be much inclination towards censorship or personal attacks to stifle debate or to censor unorthodox or original ideas in plural democracies with free speech. One might have concluded, or at least hoped, by the year 2000 that the risk of objective scientific debate being impaired by ideological, religious, or political orthodoxy was a thing of the past. Perhaps we were naïve to take this view.

The topic of climate change has been debated widely by scientists and in the mainstream media since at least the late nineteenth century. During the twentieth century, scientists theorised about whether natural climate changes and human activities were leading to a global ice age or to global warming. The scientific debate seemed to be conducted in an

open and productive manner for most of the twentieth century. Some scientists wondered whether tiny
particulate matter emitted from burning fossil fuels
might reduce global temperatures by blocking sunlight from reaching the surface of the earth. Other
scientists wondered if some gases emitted by human
activity might increase the rate of warming by preventing heat from escaping from the earth. Most
scientists in this area of study recognised the background trends in sea level and temperature changes, which date back hundreds of thousands of years,
with little influence from human activities.

Gradually, scientists reached a general understanding that there were natural cycles of warming
and cooling which repeat approximately every hundred thousand years or so due to variations in the
rotation and orbit of the earth, the distance of the
earth from the sun, and variations in activity of the
sun. The scientific debate was conducted with respect on both sides.

It is notable that the excellent, original, and unorthodox work of Nikolaus Copernicus and Galileo
Galilei had provided a solid foundation for objective
and rational understanding of the planetary and
solar cycles despite the attempts of censors to stifle
their work. If we still believed that the earth was stationary, we could not have understood how ice ages

and warm periods occurred in response to the rotation and orbits of planets and our sun. It is also interesting that the majority of mainstream philosophers across Europe in the sixteenth century opposed Copernicus and Galileo. The scientific consensus of the sixteenth century was definitely on the side of a stationary earth orbited by a sun. Fear of persecution had a chilling effect on the objective mind at that time, and we can ask ourselves if this might have the same effect in the twenty-first century.

Late in the twentieth century and early in the twenty-first century, there seemed to be a shift in the attitude of some scientists and some media publishers towards less tolerance and transparency for some ideas and theories that did not fit with their preferred orthodoxy. Perhaps the development of social media had encouraged a less polite, less tolerant, rather crude attitude amongst journalists and scientists. Perhaps there was a more organised political reason for this change—one which was linked to the promotion of socialism and opposition to capitalism. The orthodox ideas of the sixteenth century endorsed the concept of a stationary earth for religious and political reasons. Without the challenge of unorthodox or original ideas from Copernicus and Galileo, we would still be mistaken about planetary motions. Surely the scientists of the twenty-first century understood this fundamental principle of science. Surely modern scientists would avoid the temptation to fall back into a process driven by ideology.

A controversy emerged in 2009 when correspondence between academics at the University of East Anglia in southeast England revealed scientists discussing adjusting data on global temperature measurements. Adjusting scientific data is not unreasonable as long as the reason for adjustments are explicit, transparent, and objectively justified. However, falsification of data for reasons of ideology or bias is a serious and scandalous scientific mistake. Some commentators interpreted this scandal to mean that the scientists were concealing a decline in temperatures which did not fit their preferred warming theories in order to promote the idea of man-made global heating as part of a wider political project. Another controversy emerged in 2016 when a senior climate scientist in Australia was dismissed from his post, just after he had criticised the quality of data used by colleagues in his academic field of research regarding changing temperatures and coral bleaching.

Challenging the quality of research data in a polite and objective manner is one cornerstone of all scientific research. This would not normally have resulted in dismissal from a research post. The dismissed academic was described as a climate "denier" by many media journalists. A court in Australia in 2019 found that the scientist in question had been unfairly dismissed. The phrase "climate denial" or "climate denier" had been coined in the late twentieth century. It is notable that scientific debates in other less contentious areas of research, such as antibiotic development, hip transplant surgery, or silicon chip development, did not lead to terms such as "antibiotic denial," "transplant denial," or "silicon chip denier." None of the scientists who find data suggesting climate cooling have used the term "global cooling denier" or "ice age denier" to describe those who disagree with their theories.

To describe an opponent in a debate as a "subject denier" is a quite significant distance from the scientific method established over four hundred years since the Enlightenment. Scientists are supposed to test—or challenge—a theory by trying to disprove it. They are even supposed to try to disprove their own theory. Scientists traditionally encouraged opponents to challenge their theories. This is a fundamental scientific principle. Encouraging colleagues to test a theory in this way had been considered a positive part of rigorous scientific analysis. Theories which survive such challenges are generally closer to the truth than those that don't survive scrutiny.

A second example of a development that might cause concern in relation to free speech is a proposal in Britain to define Islamophobia as racist and therefore illegal under discrimination laws. This proposal selectively protects Islam against any criticism. This looks strikingly similar to stifling of criticism of the Catholic Church in the sixteenth century by the Roman Inquisition. If criticism of a religion is no longer legal, then free speech has ended.

These are just two examples amongst many which cause concern. To the observer untrained in climate science or employment law, the scandal about climate changes at the English university and the data dispute case in Australia have the outwards appearance of academics trying to stifle debate and to censor colleagues with whom they disagree. This is a more important issue than climate changes or data analysis because it threatens the fundamental basis of all science. It looks suspiciously as if ideology may have taken over in the minds of some scientists. The appearance that ideology might be driving the scientific process, rather than objective data and open debate, takes us back uncomfortably to the Roman Inquisition of the sixteenth century. Perhaps there would be some merit in asking our science students to study history a little more.

As the title of this book suggests, this story is about words, in particular the freedom we have to choose and express words (i.e., freedom of speech). This story could not have been written and would not be read without freedom of speech. The fact that you are reading it suggests that there has been some success in promoting and spreading free speech in your time and place. The author of this story did not need to seek the permission of any pope, imam, or president to publish. Anyone who criticises or praises this story will be enjoying the same freedom as the author of the story, with the encouragement of the same author. This will further reinforce the value and security of such freedom.

This story is a work of fiction, of course, and the author hopes that it remains that way, but the subject is one we should take seriously. We must never cease to proclaim the principle of freedom of speech, which is a joint inheritance of all people since the Magna Carta, through the American Declaration of Independence, to the present day and for future generations.

Political correctness is just one method of preventing free speech for political ends. Religious censorship is another method of censoring speech. As part of the natural right of free speech, all people of every country have the right to free elections with secret ballots to choose and dismiss their governments.

Noam Chomsky once wrote 'If you are really in favour of free speech, then you're in favour of freedom of speech for precisely the views you despise'. So, freedom of speech means freedom for everyone to speak, including those with whom we may disagree, because free speech is our best protection against all forms of tyranny.

THE END